Tales from Where the Wall is Cracked

Tales from Where the Wall is Cracked

Paul Bradley

Bridge House

British Library Cataloguing in Publication Data
A Record of this Publication is available from the British
Library

ISBN 978-1-907335-74-7

This edition published 2020 by Bridge House Publishing
Manchester, England

Contents

The Yellow Inspector

A quarter of a century ago I lived in a shabby ground floor bedsit by the sea. I was eighteen and had a job in a roof tile factory where my uncle was a foreman, but I had dreams of becoming a writer and attended an evening course at the local college. In the room above lived Ian Webster. I knew his full name because all the post was put on a side cupboard in the hallway for collection. He moved in just before I did. Miss Foulkes, the landlady, who looked and dressed like Margaret Thatcher, told me he was a care in the community case. He'd been settled into the locality after leaving hospital and was on some kind of anti-psychotic medication.

I saw Ian infrequently. When we passed in the corridor, coming in or out of the bathroom, or when we saw each other outside, I made a point of picking up the pace and avoiding eye contact. Not once did I say hello or nod in his direction. He wore cheap old fashioned clothes such as cardigans with zips, loose fitting dark blue jeans and shiny fake leather shoes. His pockmarked face seemed to have a yellow tinge and his teeth were dark yellow too.

Whenever I saw him he had a cigarette either in his mouth or between nicotine yellow fingers and he seemed deep in thought. Above his upper lip lived a long and startling yellowy brown moustache under deep set disheartened eyes usually facing downwards. The only thing neat about Ian was his sandy yellow hair. He pushed it habitually across his head from left to right and a couple of times I noticed he would take a black comb out of an inside jacket pocket and methodically use it whilst walking past. Yellow. That's what he was. In my mind I referred to him as the yellow man. Miss Foulkes said he was only twenty-nine, but he looked like he was well into middle age.

The truth is, I was worried about what Ian might be capable of. I'd known a lad at school whose dad wasn't well, so to speak. Apparently he had the strength of ten men, frothed at the mouth and got violent if there was a full moon. Then there was my Uncle Vince. The whole family kept quiet about him and he was never at family gatherings. There was a picture of him in one of our photo albums looking happy as a youngster at a fairground but I convinced myself he looked possessed.

I only spoke to Ian once. It was a Saturday night and I was in my room watching *Match of the Day*. There was a loud, insistent double knock on the door. Miss Foulkes was the only other person who had ever knocked and hers was a triple knock, quite gentle. I crept towards the door, but didn't open it. There was another, identical knock.

'Who is it?' I asked, voice raised because of the football commentary.

'Ian from upstairs. I've run out of cigarettes and was wondering…'

'I haven't got any. I don't smoke,' I yelled.

A short pause. 'OK. Sorry to disturb you.'

I stayed behind the door for a minute or so and listened to his steps on the stairs, along the hall and the opening and closing of the door to his room. Then I went back to my chair to watch the football and light a cigarette. He might well have seen me smoking as back then I smoked constantly. I'd been surprised by his voice – he sounded a bit posh.

The following morning I had a visit from Miss Foulkes who wanted to empty the electric meters.

'That fella from upstairs knocked on my door last night,' I said.

'What did he want?' she asked, with a hint of alarm.

'He'd run out of fags.'

'Really? He's always got a big carton on his mantelpiece.

I've just been up to empty his meter. I'm sure they were there as usual. He's an odd one that's for sure. Always reading, books everywhere. Philosophy, religion, psychology, you name it. Poor bugger should give his mind a rest.'

I didn't see Ian for some time after that. I heard him wandering around his room at odd hours of the night whilst I tried to sleep, but our paths didn't cross. One night in the summer I heard him coming downstairs. He answered the front door and there were two female Jehovah's witnesses who had come to talk to him. I'd watched them coming down the path and hoped they weren't calling on me as they had in the past. My window was half open as it was still warm out.

I had an idea. The creative writing tutor had asked the students to pay attention to everyday conversation and provide examples so I grabbed my pen and note pad, crept to the window and listened to the conversation intently, urgently scribbling and glimpsing out at the same time.

'Hi Ian. Did you read the magazine?' asked the younger woman.

'Yes,' said Ian.

'What did you think?'

'I don't believe in eternal life.'

'Why?'

'Well, it's based on belief and faith. No evidence.'

The older woman took over. 'What do you think happens when we die then? Where do our souls go?'

'What is the soul?' asked Ian.

'Well, it's the spirit.'

'What is the spirit?' asked Ian.

'It's our life force. God controls it. If we believe and live good lives God can turn the spirit back on and give us everlasting life.'

'Sorry, I don't believe it,' said Ian.

'You think we just die and that's it? Isn't that pointless?'

'Not at all.'

'How do you think we got here? Who created us Ian?'

'I've got no idea. I just know we're here.'

'Surely you want answers?

'I'm OK without them. Why don't you come inside? I'll make you both a cup of tea.'

'That would be nice. Thank you Ian.'

I sat down and rewrote my barely legible notes. I passed his views off as a madman's ranting. What could the yellow man possibly know about God and eternal life? I shared the conversation with the writing class and my tutor said the conversation was unusual in its precision and formality when written down but context explains why this is so.

Soon after, I left both the factory and bedsit and moved briefly back to my parents' house. I'd spent the last year as a 'reject man', ejecting faulty roof tiles off a production line, and the experience had made me ambitious. I quit writing, started a management course and ended up in a good position with a multinational based in the city. Next came marriage, a semi-detached in suburbia, kids, divorce, access to the kids, re-marriage. My life revolved around drink, making money, promotion, driving nice cars, deadlines, sales targets, meetings and family. In that order. People have fallen into two categories; those who are useful to me and those who aren't.

In all those years I can't remember thinking about Ian. There was no need. About a year ago, however, I came across him again, indirectly, on my way from Manchester to London on the train to attend a dull marketing conference. I was travelling first class nursing a hangover. I'd loosened my tie, stretched, ordered coffee and lazily turned on my laptop so that I could read the conference agenda and fool myself that I was working. The topic bored me so I read the paper instead.

After glancing at the headlines I turned the page and, casually at first, read about a coroner's verdict of suicide in relation to the death of Ian Webster at his bedsit in a seaside town. He had been found after a fellow resident at the property reported an overpowering smell. His body was in an advanced state of decomposition when found by the emergency services. That same resident was quoted in the papers, 'Ian kept himself to himself and it was not unusual to go some time without seeing him.' The article went on to point out that Ian had suffered a long-term mental illness and had been isolated in the community for many years, moving frequently. Questions were raised about the failure of care in the community as a policy. Lack of funds, lack of supervision, lack of everything. There was a grainy old picture of Ian as a much younger man next to the write up.

I put my paper down, looked out of the window. Towns, fields, farms, rivers and roads blurred past, but all I saw was Ian standing behind my door asking for cigarettes or combing his yellow hair. The previous weekend I'd been to see an amateur production of *An Inspector Calls* with my wife. I imagined an inspector knocking at my door, questioning me. Except this inspector was yellow.

'Is it true you refused Mr Webster a cigarette, told him lies and did not answer the door to him?'

'Yes. He was a complete lunatic and had his own fags.'

'Did it ever occur to you that you might at least have said hello to Ian Webster?'

'I was so much younger then. It's not as if I actively went out of my way to upset him.'

'True. But it isn't what you did Mr. Clarke. It's what you didn't do. It's what everybody didn't, doesn't or will

10

not do. That's the whole point. We are responsible for each other. What would you do now?'

'Look, it wasn't my fault. We've all got our own lives to live. I've sorted my life out why didn't he? It's a fight for survival. The authorities let him down not me. Still, I'd probably give him a fag now, so I can't be that bad. I'd buy him a pack. I quit years ago.'

I started reading my paper again. It was a relief to turn to the sports pages but I felt resentful when I got off the train. On the way to the conference I came across a *Big Issue* vendor and the yellow inspector appeared again. 'Well?' he said. I told him silently where to go in no uncertain terms and looked at the vendor like I wanted to kill him. Probably spends his money on beer and drugs anyway.

Since then things have gone downhill. My wife and I split up and I started smoking again, very heavily too. The inspector encouraged me, saying it would help me deal with the stress, though keeping the yellow off my teeth and smoking fingers is a constant struggle. The inspector also persuaded me to drink even more just when I was finally admitting to myself that I needed to sober up. He said it would calm me down and a few drinks never hurt anyone. I've now been diagnosed with alcoholic liver disease. Symptoms? Fatigue, vomiting and jaundice. The whites of my eyes have turned yellow and so has my skin. One of my more jocular work colleagues sent me an e-mail informing me that 'Everyone sends best wishes to the yellow man'. The consultant reckons most of the damage to my liver could be reversible at this stage if I quit drinking and I'm pleased to say the inspector seems to be pointing me in the right direction but it's far from easy. I've had plenty of relapses and feel as though I'm going out of my mind half the time.

Recently, I was going through my belongings after I'd

moved out of the family home. I came across the old note pad I'd used to record Ian's conversation with the Jehovah's Witnesses. I was about to throw it away when the inspector, yellower, more insistent and everywhere suggested I start writing again and to begin with a story about Ian Webster.

The Conference

Mr Oliver Hughes arrived at Euston station on the early train. He was wearing his best business suit and, briefcase in hand, scurried across the station platform like a wind-up toy powered by Duracell. The conference was due to start in twenty minutes, and, although it was only a short walk up North Gower Street, he needed to be seen to arrive on time.

Keeping up with the crowd, it struck Mr Hughes even more keenly than usual just how similar his situation was to many others amongst the well-dressed corporate pack he jostled with. They were also escaping the platform as if their lives depended on it, heads up and forward, clasping briefcases and bags, speaking urgently on phones. Mr Hughes wondered, momentarily, if they might be half way through mortgages, with functional marriages and children to support through university just like him. And here they all were heading into the slow drizzle of London for another day of deals, meetings, deadlines and networking.

Over at the conference, Mr Hughes signed in and settled into his seat with a coffee. He read the conference agenda half-heartedly, reading glasses perched on the bridge of his nose. The whole day was dedicated to the stabilising and enhancing of company profits during a recession. Another day, he thought, of feigned interest in order to service his commitments and debts. He noted the times for coffee breaks, lunch, and the whereabouts of a number of attractive women he'd clocked on arrival.

The first conference speaker was a professorial middle-aged man with a small rounded paunch. He was briefly introduced before inflicting a version of death on the attendees by reading slavishly off his PowerPoint notes as if his corporate life depended on it. Something about seeking new markets, product placement and the need to replace existing models of management in the current economic climate. Mr Hughes fell asleep with his eyes open and a head full of questions. How much of themselves do attendees, including himself, invest in corporate life? To what extent does the maintenance of corporate profits and growth define anybody's sense of who they are? Do other people at this conference ask themselves these questions?

Tiny beads of sweat were beginning to pump slowly out of the speaker's high forehead. Even his hunched silhouette looked vulnerable up on the screen. Mr Hughes smiled. The poor fellow just wants to eat, drink, sleep and laugh and he ends up doing this to keep it all going. It was as painful to witness as it surely was to do and for some reason Mr Hughes wondered what the speaker does in his spare time to resist such intrusions into everyday life. What do people do to fight back, to reclaim a sense of who they are?

Maybe the speaker enjoys sitting in a cosy bird hide at weekends with an old tartan flask of tea, corned beef sandwiches and binoculars. Yes, the contrast between office life and the great outdoors might work for this chap, all those wide open spaces, fresh air and birdsong. Or maybe he has a train set in his loft that he's been adding to for years with little porters, station masters, signal boxes, bridges, trees and ever expanding towns. At that point, however, Mr Hughes noted something a little unusual about the speaker. He was wearing a Harley Davidson belt with the logo prominent on the buckle. The very words conjured up images for Mr Hughes of wild outlaw motorcycle gangs, freedom of the highway, *Easy Rider*. Surely this guest speaker, with his monochrome suit and monotone voice, could not possibly ride a Harley.

The image of the speaker riding a Harley soon gave way to another question in the mind of the thoughtful Mr

Hughes. The issue that concerned him now was why the speaker wore the belt. He will have known that he was giving a certain impression of himself counter to that of a corporate functionary. There was possibly a hint of danger about him and the belt may signify the speaker's desire to mildly project a certain image, a distancing between whom we see and who he really is. Mr Hughes couldn't know this for sure, but it seemed to make some kind of sense. A certain smugness accompanied these observations.

Looking discreetly around at nearby attendees, Mr Hughes noticed other idiosyncrasies. He recognised one woman vaguely. She worked in a separate department at the company he worked for. She had long mousy hair and a faint bohemian style with a tattoo above her wrist, just visible beneath the wavy arm of her colourful paisley blouse. It looked like it might be a Celtic band but this was not obvious. Next he noticed a small CND sticker on a briefcase. There seemed to be something a little different about everyone he looked at. Some attendees sat upright with studied concentration on their faces whilst others seemed to adopt an overtly relaxed deportation as if to signify some kind of cool detachment.

A crescendo of hand clapping shifted Mr Hughes' attention. The speaker was finished, the next one introduced and more PowerPoint appeared on the screen, this time with sound, colour and zooming in functions. It was a PowerPoint spectacular. The speaker, a smartly dressed woman in her late twenties, positively sparkled. She alternated the pitch of her voice and emphasised certain words and points. Her hand movements and facial expressions captured meaning effortlessly. She oozed confidence and style. At relevant points humour was employed with little gaps after the punch line for appreciation from the audience. Questions were welcomed. She kept eye contact with all attendees in turn, making them feel personally addressed. This, Mr Hughes realised, was a performance, and a highly impressive one at that. Her topic was staff motivation. She wore a classic black trouser suit with a frilly white blouse and her hair was healthy and shiny. What an impressive woman. Mr Hughes studied her closely. Her routine, delivered with such poise was almost flawless.

She added a little humour to her closing comments and waited, again, for audience appreciation. However, on this occasion, there was no laughter. No one seemed to quite realise they were supposed to laugh. The speaker moved from one foot to another, mumbling something inaudible before reaching quickly for the button to move onto the final slide. It was only a blip, hardly noticeable. The presentation soon ended to a rapturous and well deserved applause which the speaker was clearly very happy to receive.

Mr Hughes considered the blip. It seemed to him that the speaker may have chosen to approach her task the way she did because she needed the certainty of a well-established routine. She had needed to know exactly what and how to deliver her material and her confidence was dependent upon the successful implementation of her strategy. The blip unnerved her temporarily and she momentarily lost her anchor, revealing the panic underneath. To what extent, Mr Hughes wondered, was the speaker really immersed in her role? Had she dreaded the performance, despite the poised conviction of its delivery? Was there once a time, maybe in a school play in primary school long ago, when she had fluffed her lines and faced admonishment for doing so? Had the striving for perfection increased her sense of individuality or led to a robotic version of it in a vulnerable search for acceptance?

Mr Hughes didn't know the answers but he was beginning to feel overly judgemental. As the last guest speaker before coffee break got under way, he decided to focus on himself. He checked his watch discreetly. It was tucked away from view beneath his shirt sleeve beyond the buttoned cuff of his left wrist. It was a child's watch and it had belonged to his son, Joel, when he was around six or seven. Mr Hughes had found it at the bottom of an old toy box in the attic that he had been sorting through one weekend about a year before. It was well over ten years since it had been in use but Mr Hughes tried a new battery and found it still worked. The watch face was a big, beaming Mickey Mouse whose thin arms and big pointing fingers told the time. What did the wearing of this watch reveal about himself, Mr Hughes wondered.

It was the first watch he had bought for his son and he remembered how proud Joel had been that Christmas day when he opened it as a present. He wore it to school, in bed, anywhere they went and would often be seen just gazing at it on his wrist. Mr Hughes recalled happy times at that stage of fatherhood. It was well before the closed bedroom door stage, thrash heavy metal, Facebook, the stunted communication of the teenage years and the endless disagreements. The watch represented the innocence of that time.

But that didn't explain why Mr Hughes chose to wear it at work. In fact, the more he thought about it, the more he realised, or convinced himself, that the watch represented his own desire to reclaim his childhood. Those days had been tough and he'd had to grow up very quickly. He was only nine when his parents got divorced and his mother brought him up along with his brother and sister in a council house. He was the eldest and from an early age he had helped his mother around the house and increasingly looked after his siblings as he got older. It wasn't the worst childhood. His father was in constant touch and his mother did her best but he always had some responsibility and there was very little money. Mr Hughes had bought Joel and his daughter, Nia, many toys, games and films and spent hours with them playing, making sure the magic of childhood wonder could be theirs. He had given them what he felt he had never truly had as a child and now they were older, at university, he wore the watch as a symbol of something that had been lost. He wanted to be that little boy at heart just like Joel had been.

Mr Hughes started to feel a little satisfied with himself. There was certainly some truth in his pondering. There was a sense, however, though he was loathe to admit it, that he had over placed the watch at the centre of his own life drama and purposefully built a narrative around it so that he could emerge as some kind of hero. He had sacrificed his childhood and then made sure his own children lived the dream and now he wore the watch as some kind of medal or reminder of his selfless service. Mr Hughes knew this account, this interpretation of history, was very much in keeping with his personality. Acts of kindness always served to boost his own sense of self-worth. He was also prone to self-pity. He'd had plenty of toys as a child and, though times were undoubtedly tough, there had been plenty of lightness in his childhood. As for the watch, the wearing of it demanded a little more consideration.

Mr Hughes, now more honest with himself, realised he wore the watch for work because he thought of himself as quirky. He liked to look at his watch and check the time when he knew others would notice. They would see the watch and recognise he was somehow different. He didn't need an expensive timepiece to confirm his worth. Underneath this reliable, middle management exterior was a person who knows who he really is. Most of his adult life, he realised, had been spent distancing himself from others. *They* were all salary slaves, *they* were conformists, and *they* were the nuts and bolts of a dreary, never ending false consciousness. *They* had been taken in by money, things, advertisements that manufactured new desires, *they* had sold themselves out to 'the system', and *they* perpetuated it. *They* believed in the promise of love, advancement, progress, aspirations, moral codes and a bright new future.

The problem, Mr Hughes was slowly beginning to realise, with his Mickey Mouse watch and his unique outlook, was that he was exactly the same. He wore the watch to remind himself and others that he hadn't quite been crushed, that he retained a distinct identity. It gave him a boyish charm, he thought. But then he looked back to his university days. All those dreams of transforming the world, anti-nuclear bomb marches, smoky gatherings of hairy utopian socialists, radical feminist speeches at the student union, legalise marijuana demonstrations. Now he had been reduced to wearing an iconic symbol of a vast entertainment corporation on his wrist to represent his sense of distance from the status quo. Quirky Mr Hughes. The ex-radical with a gold American express card.

The speaker finished talking and it was coffee break. Mr Hughes decided to have a quick chat with the paisley-wearing woman with the Celtic style tattoo. After some small talk he asked her what the tattoo meant to her. She said that it meant nothing, and that the constant search for meaning in external reality was leading to a vacuum in our inner lives. She handed Mr Hughes a card as she was starting up meditation and mindfulness classes as a side-line. It would help people to reconnect with the present and provide a useful extra income to help meet her daughter's university costs. She was offering a fee reduction to work colleagues.

Mr Hughes silently considered the views of this enthusiastic salesperson for the Buddha. He had already been to a similar class in the recent past. During his final meditation session, the group had been asked to silently contemplate the slow trickle of a dew drop down the surface of a drooping lotus leaf. When it ended, the kindly Buddhist monk had asked the class members if they had been able to focus their 'intrusive butterfly minds'. Mr Hughes had told her that he had recently been issued a speeding ticket and all he could think about was murdering the chief constable and anyone who looked like him. The only idea he'd been able to relate to was the slowness of it. He had committed his murders very slowly.

Mr Hughes rang his boss, telling him he had a migraine and would have to go home. His boss was understanding but concerned as Mr Hughes had had a number of migraines recently. As he wandered through the drizzle into Euston station Mr Hughes was met by an army of suits heading for the exit from a disembarked train.

It felt good to be worming his way through them in the opposite direction.

The Dark Side of my Moon

Last summer I went to Rhyl to buy a pair of shoes and found what I wanted quickly. It was a sunny day so I enjoyed a wander along the promenade, weaving between tattooed holidaymakers, past the noisy amusement arcades, bingo halls, donut sellers, fancy goods shops and full beer gardens. With time to spare I headed for the fun fair in a wave of childhood nostalgia. The music was blasting from the bumper car ride and the kids screamed in gleeful terror as the roller coaster took its first big dip. I was about to leave when I came across a sign near the ghost train:

CONSULT GYPSY ROMANA TODAY
NEXT TO FAIRGROUND
in the Springfield Arcade
CELEBRITY PSYCHIC
TV PERSONALITY
CRYSTAL BALL & TAROT READINGS
FROM £10

I headed over to the Arcade and found a small wooden hut at the back near the pool tables. It seemed really small from the outside and on the front were hand written testimonies to Gypsy Romana's visionary practise, along with fading black and white photos of her with 'stars' from the world of entertainment posing outside her hut, or, oddly, on a boat. The 'stars' looked old fashioned and unfamiliar although I felt a vague sense of recognition with regards at least one of them. I gave the door three quick loud thumps. A faint, broken and ancient voice, a bit creepy, immediately commanded, 'Come in! Come in!' I hesitated before entering a dim, candlelit, surprisingly spacious lair. Gypsy

21

Romana was sat behind a round table with sumptuous red and gold cloth draped over it towards the floor. In the middle was a large crystal ball seated on a black velvet cushion and, on Gypsy Romana's side, a set of tarot cards, smoky incense burner, glass of water, packet of king size cigarettes, lighter and ashtray.

I took a closer look at Gypsy Romana once my eyes adjusted to the shadowy gloom. She wore a burgundy head scarf and dangling gold loop earrings between an angular bronzed wrinkled face with round glasses perched in the middle of a crooked nose. Her turquoise eyes were ageless and luminous. She took a good look at me, beckoning me to sit down with a dismissive hand gesture.

'Your name?' she asked in a tone that was now withering and higher pitched.

'John,' I apologised.

'Tarot or crystal ball?'

'Well, I've never done anything like this before so I'm not sure.'

Gypsy Romana just sat there sizing me up.

'I think I'll go for the crystal ball. Do you mind if I call you Miss Rom-?'

'Ten pound for a half hour consultation with the crystal ball. Cash up front.'

I handed her the tenner and she dropped it brusquely into a wicker basket at her side. In one terse movement she removed her gaze and leant forward towards the crystal ball, immediately concentrating hard. Nothing was said for a long five minutes. Her facial expressions alternated between disgust, smiles, confusion, and surprise. Impatiently, I looked closely into the crystal ball but could only see through it onto the velvet cushion base and the cloth over the table.

'What can you s-?' I tried to ask.

'Ssshh.'

Gypsy Romana peered over her glasses and gave me a look the like of which I hadn't experienced since I was a young lad. I shifted restlessly in my seat as a mild act of defiance. Gypsy Romana began to hover her bony bejewelled fingers around the crystal ball.

'Are you local?' she asked.

'Yes.'

'Any children?'

'No.'

'Are you a comedian?'

'No. Why?'

'Slim women with dark hair will find you very funny in the near future.'

'Really? Women usually ignore me regardless of their appearance. Any romance?'

'I've told you what I know.'

Gypsy Romana placed a cigarette in a long purple holder that seemed to appear from her sleeve and lit up. I moved my head back but she exhaled a cloud of blue smoke in my direction anyway. Removing her glare, she stubbed out the cigarette and leant towards the crystal ball again, this time circling her twisted hands rhythmically like she was massaging the air around its surface. I could hear the distant scream of the kids on the big dipper. A moment passed before she spoke slowly after gradually leaning back, as if the information had been fought for.

'In the near future you will be going abroad to somewhere you have always wanted to go,' she said.

'Oh. I usually go to Skegness on holiday,' I replied.

That look. Again.

'Your money situation will improve due to unforeseen circumstances,' she said.

I didn't bother to tell her that my money situation was fine, that I had a few quid saved up. She was just picking out clues, covering the usual stuff. I'm scruffy, wear ill-fitting clothing and I'm unshaven. I certainly don't look prosperous and most people hope for financial improvements. Unexpectedly, Gypsy Romana revealed a sinister smile. Her eyes widened and glistened as she lowered her tone to a deep crackly whisper whilst staring intently at the crystal ball. For the first time she looked delighted.

'I can see an ominous dark shadow dancing across the moon,' she said.

'Er, what exactly does that mean?'

'Are you in good health?'

'Well, my grapes, I mean my haemorrhoids, can play up at times. Maybe the moon is my backside. Am I right?'

'The reading is over.'

'Hold on. I'm not going to die am I?'

'We are all going to die. Reading over.'

The dismissive wave of a hand discouraged further enquiry. I went straight for the door and into the arcade without saying goodbye. As I weaved back along the promenade and headed for my car I felt a bit foolish. Driving home I shelved the experience and within a week my visit to Gypsy Romana had been largely forgotten.

The following month, August, I went to Skegness for my annual holiday. Same caravan, same dates, same journey, different year. My haemorrhoids misbehaved terribly, bleeding and itching continually. I had to change my underwear three times a day and I bought some cream to ease the itching. When I returned home I went to see my GP. She referred me to the botty consultant at the hospital. In the meantime I received a generous inheritance from my dear Aunty Florence who had recently died following an unfortunate incident whilst ten pin bowling. By all accounts she had forgotten to let go of the bowl after the run up. I decided to spend some of the cash on a trip to India the following year as I'd always fancied it. I was still unwilling to credit Gypsy Romana with anything other than decent guess work at this stage.

A month went by before I received the appointment to see the consultant, a middle aged man called Mr Hemitch. I was ushered into his consulting room by an attractive nurse, slim with dark hair. I wondered how many unhealthy arses they had seen and if any stood out. He asked me questions about my diet, how often I passed blood, any stomach pains and so on. Next, he requested I lie on a plinth in a sideways position with my back facing him whilst he put on some disposable gloves. I then had to drop my trousers and undies to my ankles and bend my legs, so that he could lubricate my sore anus in preparation for a probing medical instrument to view my insides.

Just as I was poised to receive it Mr Hemitch addressed me in a plumy drawl. 'Are you aware, Mr Thomas, that you have a bar code on your backside?'

'A barcode? What do you mean Doctor, sorry, Mr Hemitch?'

Mr Hemitch gently eased a price tag off my exposed left arse cheek. He leant over and placed said item in front of my eyes. It was on the end of his right middle finger. I half turned my head around and saw him indicate to the nurse to put a finger out. He passed the sticker on and she wandered across the room to dispose of it. Mr Hemitch looked at me with eyebrows raised, inviting an explanation.

'As you've seen I'm only worth a pound. Next time scan me,' I suggested.

He carried on with the examination silently. I had been lying naked on the settee at home before getting ready and must have sat on a sticky price tag. I could hear the nurse suppressing giggles and found myself joining in, careful not to move my backside too much.

Mr Hemitch informed me that I had an acute multiple haemorrhoid condition and that I would be hearing from the hospital within a few weeks. As I was leaving I sheepishly said 'Goodbye' to the nurse. She winked before recommending that next time I make sure I'm worth at least a fiver. I promised that in future my backside would be a bar code free zone.

A few weeks later I received a pre-op appointment. I had to go in and have a barium meal so that the medical team could examine my stools and x-ray my insides. It involved taking the liquid, waiting a while and then being x-rayed whilst emptying my bowels. This was a bizarre experience as it was all displayed on a screen and I could see the physical act from the inside as it were; the movement of the intestines, the opening of the anus and the elimination of white waste not dissimilar in shade to dog poo from the 1970's.

After doing the business and putting my pyjamas back on I was given some temporary padding for my ring piece along with a flimsy blue apron, then taken onto the ward and told to lie down. On the way I picked up a two year old copy of Cosmopolitan off a chair. I pulled the curtains around my bed and started to read an article about why women don't like beards. Apparently it's a hygiene issue. As soon as I found this out a gorgeous middle-aged nurse, slim with dark hair, came through the gap in the curtains and said I needed to put on another pad to prevent leakage. In one hand she held an extremely large light green disposable nappy. I said 'Oh, OK,' and arched my back a bit and started to raise my big white legs into the air to make it easier. She looked confused.

'No Mr Thomas, I'm not going to put it on for you. You need to go to the bathroom and do it yourself.'

'Oh, I'm sorry,' I said.

I took the large man nappy to the bathroom. As I walked

past the reception desk on the way back I could hear nurses in the staff room at the back laughing raucously. I lay on my bed in that nappy for an hour before the nurse came back.

'You can leave now Mr Thomas, after you've got changed.'

'Shall I take this nappy off first?'

'It's up to you, but you'll have to take it off yourself.'

'Shame. I was hoping you'd talc my botty before I go. I pay my taxes.'

She chuckled. I went to the bathroom to get changed and out of there after placing my nappy in the hygienic disposal bin under the sink.

The operation date arrived and I'd arranged ten days off work as recommended. I was wheeled down to the theatre via a large lift by a heavily tattooed porter who didn't speak. After being put under anaesthetic my grapes were removed by laser. What an image. An assistant will have held open my mud flaps as the surgeon took aim. For all I knew they were all dressed as Jedi knights and used a lightsaber. I came round surrounded by two nurses in the recovery bay and I burst into a crazed diatribe about cheese sandwiches before being wheeled back to the ward by the same dull porter. I stayed overnight because my backside was like a blood orange. I was given a number of pads to change into when necessary and some tights to put over the top and keep it all together.

The consultant discharged me the following afternoon whilst on his ward round with three curious young trainees. He encouraged me to spend less time on the loo and eat plenty of fruit and vegetables. The nurses fixed me up with powdered laxative drinks to make it easier to go to the toilet for a week or so and also gave me some smaller white pads, more tights, painkillers and soothing cream in case I needed to cool down my ring piece. I thanked them for everything and drove home despite being advised to avoid driving for a while.

It was a peculiar week lying in bed wearing my nappy, tights, pads and pyjamas. I caught up on some reading and watched old Boris Karloff movies and Columbo repeats. The only real discomfort came after going to the toilet. Even though the stools were soft the pain had a sharp sting that lasted.

One afternoon I went to the toilet and suffered a movement of such ferocity that it left my ring piece throbbing in rebellion. I clenched my arse cheeks together and held onto the bathroom sink begging the pain to disappear. It wouldn't. I took some painkillers from the bathroom cabinet, swallowed them and hoped they would work instantly. They didn't. Next I reached for the soothing cream. Seizing it, I applied a large quantity gently around my smarting piece. Within a second my arse felt like Johnny Cash's *Ring of Fire*. I looked in the mirror and cried out loud 'Aaaaarghhh my bloody ring piece' before running around my flat with arse cheeks clenched like a vice, waddling like a penguin, effing and jeffing. The only thing I could think of doing was to run a cold bath and lower my piece slowly in the water in the hope it would cool things down a bit. Sweat pumped from my forehead. Fortunately the cold water did the trick and I lay there for a good ten minutes staring at some weird curly damp fungus on the cracked ceiling as the pain subsided. After carefully drying off I went to the bathroom cabinet to take a look at the cream I'd used so liberally. The tube had the following words on it:

Menthol foot balm. Absorbs rapidly

The cream from the hospital was in a similar tube. I went for a lie down on the sofa and it was then that I thought back to Gypsy Romana. I remembered that wicked smile when she talked about a dark shadow dancing across the moon and how I'd dismissed it all as nonsense.

A month after the operation I was back in Rhyl, shopping.

28

The fair was now closed for the winter but curiosity found me back at the Springfield Arcade which was open all year round. I went over to where Gypsy Romana's hut had been but all I found was fruit machines, a mechanical horse race and the pool tables. I asked the young woman in the change booth if she knew where I might find the gypsy fortune teller. She continued counting coins before nonchalantly replying in a strong scouse accent, 'There's been no gypsy here Mister.'

'There was last summer. Over there at the back of the pool tables,' I said.

'I've been here two years. No gypsy,' she insisted.

Mystified, I went to the fun fair to see if I could see the sign offering Gypsy Romana's services near the ghost train. The fun fair was deserted and all the rides were under cover and lifeless like hibernating machines. No smells of hot dogs and candy floss and the only noises came from the arcade's thump a crocodile with a hammer game and seagulls mocking overhead. Over at the ghost train there was no sign.

Wandering back along the promenade I decided to head for the library to consult the local history section where I found a book covering the period 1950's-1970's. Gypsy Romana died in the summer of 1963 and had been a popular though feisty member of the community whose occasional appearances on television encouraged local tourism. She gave much of her money to local charities when she was alive and left most of it to a hospice in her will. An extract from her obituary in the local paper recounted her insistent claim that she would visit the town after her death in spirit form, extracting money from misers to benefit her favoured charities. The author gave numerous examples of alleged 'sightings' of Gypsy Romana by locals over the years and claims that she continued to read fortunes to unsuspecting visitors to the town.

Her fortune telling practise had been situated at Springfield Arcade but it was an indoor market in her day. In the early 1970s it was converted to amusements with the name retained. Two photographs of Gypsy Romana were included. In one, which I vaguely recognised from my own visit, she is with the comedian and actor Norman Wisdom. In the other she is with a singer called Lita Roza on a boat which the caption explained belonged to and was named after Gypsy Romana.

On the way back to the car I leant on the blue railings that stand along the sea wall. Small colourful anchored boats bobbed around the small misty harbour. I could just make out some of the names if they were sideways on such as Moody Blue, Sea Serpent, and The Mermaid. One boat, the furthest, turned its engine on and started to move so I put twenty pence in the telescope at my side to catch its name before it turned past the breakwater towards the rolling waves and out to sea. I focused in and almost immediately saw the words 'Gypsy Romana'. Through the window of the cab a faint robed hand appeared, waving towards the shore. I watched the boat disappear into the ever after.

0 Bootable Partition in Table

Consultant Psychiatrist Dr Jennifer Williams felt tired. Her hair was still shower wet and she ached after walking up Snowdon with her irritating husband over the weekend. She wanted a divorce and didn't feel like talking to patients. There was a new one on the ward this blustery Monday morning, a gentleman called Mr Howard Jeffries. He had been found doing something disturbing the previous Friday. Disturbing and dangerous.

Dr Williams received a briefing from the nurses and scanned Mr Jeffries' medical notes before seeing him. No record, at this stage, of any previous referral to psychiatric services. Forty-nine, works as head of a car parts sales team, grown up children, divorced, estranged from family. Articulate, reluctant to mix with other patients, laughs randomly for no apparent reason. Compliant with care and meds over the weekend. Eating and sleeping well. Smoker. Did not resist admittance under section, but on arrival was laughing hysterically and sobbing at intervals.

Howard Jeffries, a thin, rangy man, was sitting legs crossed and thoughtful in a small light green open lounge after breakfast. He wore hospital pyjamas, a dressing gown, slippers, and an identity band around his left wrist. Across the ward, patients were shouting, shuffling, demanding help, cigarettes, or sitting quietly watching TV. Dr Williams checked she had her personal alarm and, with a staff nurse, went over to introduce herself. 'Hello Mr Jeffries. I'm Dr Williams. This is my colleague, Mr Watson. Pleased to meet you. I was wondering if you could join us for a chat somewhere more private.'

'Sure,' said Mr Jeffries, offering his hand as he rose.

They entered a small assessment room through a door that opened both ways. It comprised a long table secured to the floor, blue plastic chairs and a large dull wooden framed canvas painting of flowers in a vase slightly lop sided, secured to the wall. Howard sat opposite Dr Williams while Mr Watson sat to one side, closer to the door and observation panel. Dr Williams began the assessment process. 'How are you Mr Jeffries?' she asked.

'Please call me Howard. I'm fine. No problems.'

'Good. That's really good Howard. I'm interested in learning more about the events that led up to your admittance. Have you ever done anything like that before?'

Howard smiled mischievously. 'Never. Neither had the guts or imagination.'

'Can you tell me what happened?' asked Dr Williams.

'You mean, what was going through my mind? The events that led to the incident or the incident itself?'

Howard laughed manically. His eyes were wide, but there was no hint of menace. Dr Williams did not wish to collude so her facial expression remained fixed into a kindly, concerned concentration. She kept her tone soft. 'I think we'll start with the events that led up to the incident.' Howard's laughter abruptly ceased following a short cough. 'It's difficult to explain but if you're willing to listen I'm willing to talk,' he said. 'I'm ready,' said Dr Williams.

Placing hands behind head, Howard stretched his long legs forward at an angle to avoid touching the doctor, crossed his bony feet and, looking out of the window dealt with a few preliminaries. 'Don't expect an easy explanation. It's not like that. I wasn't abused as a kid. I've no delusions, paranoid ideations or anything. It was one day and one response at that particular time though a general sense of, shall we say, world-weariness has been brewing for some time. I can't deny that. Really, do you want all of it or an edited version for ease of reference? The edited version might make me easier to categorize, you know, borderline personality disorder or whatever. The full version will take longer and your hair will be dry by the time I finish.'

Dr Williams was more than mildly surprised and she exchanged a quick glance with Mr Watson. It was unusual for her patients to use clinical terms. She wondered if this gave an indication that Howard may have been admitted to a similar hospital elsewhere in the past or had a family member who'd been through the system. Maybe he had some work experience in the field. It was noteworthy. Irrespective, Dr Williams was unused to patients setting the parameters. 'Well, I have twenty minutes now, but we could always talk more later,' she said.

'Okay. Twenty minutes should get us started. Shall I begin?' asked Howard.

'Yes Mr Jeff... err, Howard. Please go ahead.'

'I was lying in bed staring at the ceiling last Friday morning. I hadn't slept all night. There was traffic noise so I knew it was time to get up for work. I live alone. I cut my face to ribbons with a rusty razor, ate a three day old slice of take away pizza for breakfast, smoked, dressed and got in the car. Why the detail? Just to emphasize there was nothing unusual. I often don't sleep and I live a bachelor's life. I took the slow route, avoiding the motorway. I saw a flattened badger near the side of the road and two magpies nibbling at it in-between oncoming cars. It made me laugh. I suppose that was a bit odd. I laughed more than usual.'

Dr Williams raised an eyebrow. She was about to ask a question but Howard anticipated her thoughts. 'Why did I laugh? I wondered if the magpies were friends or if they would eat each other if either one of them got hit. I've always had a sick sense of humour, but for some reason it's generally confined to animals. I read about a butcher who sold rabbit meat. He put up a sign that said "Watership Down. You've read the book. You've seen the movie. Now eat the cast!" The RSPCA were involved. Laugh? I couldn't stop. And recently I read about a type of fungus in South American forests that spreads its spores towards passing marcher ants. The ants eat the spore, turn into zombies and their last act is to take a bite out of a leaf. Then they die and the fungus grows through the ants' heads and spreads more spores so the cycle continues.'

At this point Howard had to stop talking. He started laughing again, harder, and this time his eyes creased as if he was picturing the scene. He managed to compose himself before singing 'All things bright and beautiful, all creatures great and small.' There was more laughter and it seemed to feed on itself. Eventually, as he calmed down, he spluttered, 'Forgive me Dr Williams. Don't worry, I've never found human suffering particularly funny.'

Dr Williams wondered if her patient was telling the truth. Lack of compassion for the suffering of animals could be indicative of a similar lack in relation to people. However, this may not be so easy to admit and the word 'particularly' kept her interested. 'Howard, do you read the papers or watch the news?'

'Yes, both. I'm a current affairs junkie.'

'What do you think of all the things going on in the world?'

'Like I said, Dr Williams, my sick humour is confined to animals. I feel the same way as other people about the Tsunami in Japan and the riots in the Middle East.'

'And how do people feel about those events?' Dr Williams asked.

'They think they should feel sorry so they tell each other how terrible it all is. In this way they feel better. A donation to charity helps. It makes the news spectacular to watch and a kind of awkward pleasure. It reminds people of movies. Also, there is often a guilty sense of relief that whatever happened hasn't happened to yourself.'

'Is that how *you* respond to these events?' At this early stage Dr Williams reasoned she may as well be up front with her questions. She already sensed her patient was as sharp as flint. Howard, meanwhile, was beginning to enjoy himself.

'I respond in a similar way, but you're on the wrong track. I do have feelings I just don't express false ones. I've never harmed animals, I just find them funny. Their shapes and the things they do. Ridiculous! I feel all the emotions like anyone else. You know, jealousy, love, sadness, hatred, anger, joy. I know all about empathy. Some chap has just written a book about it, I read about in the paper. He reckons there is a part of the brain that deals with empathy and this may not be fully developed in some people and that's why they do awful things. Also, brain chemicals are involved. That might be so, but I think we learn to display empathy. We feel what we think we should feel and by doing so and expressing it we hope others will feel for us when we need them to. Human beings are calculating. For my part, regardless of any theory, I feel the world very closely in my own way Dr Williams and that in itself could be an issue. Shall I continue with my day?'

'Please do. You were on your way to work and you saw the dead badger…'

'That's it. The dead badger and the magpies. Like a metaphor for something, but I'm unsure what. Capitalism maybe, life, but my thoughts were vague then, as they often are. I always feel at the cusp of understanding. I carried on driving and came across a large queue waiting for a new Aldi's branch to open. There were hundreds waiting for the opening offers. All these people and it was a major event, like their lives would now be complete. I wondered how their lives got this small. Then I admitted I too was looking forward to seeing if the new store was cheaper than Asda.

It's certainly closer. It's like being angry when stuck in a traffic jam and then realizing that you're part of it. Does that make sense?'

'Erm, yes, I think so,' said Dr Williams.

'Anyway, I carried on driving and noticed the big red church on the edge of town had covered its notice board with posters. For some reason I felt compelled to stop the car, get out, and read those posters carefully.'

'What did they say? Can you remember?' Dr Williams asked.

'Yes. "Jesus will calm the storm or calm you in the storm." Also, "Sorrow is better than laughter for by the sadness of the face the heart is made better." The usual stuff.'

Dr Williams wondered if there was any relationship between the church signs and the events of Howard's day. A famous hymn had already been sung in the interview and religion, which can make people do all sorts, might be a fruitful line of enquiry. 'What did you make of the signs Howard? What significance did they have to you?'

'Inconsequential in one way but significant in another. I don't believe in God. The signs were displayed, I think, because they resonate with the Japanese tsunami. Only the day before I'd listened to a debate on the radio where religious types were saying major disasters give mankind the opportunity to demonstrate kindness. God, in his infinite wisdom, gives us that opportunity. God allows a young baby to be swept away from his family so the rest of us, from the comfort of our armchairs, can demonstrate kindness. It makes no sense. Global empathy directed by the lord in heaven for the betterment of mankind. The signs did affect me, no doubt, but they didn't fill me with religious fervour. They filled me with a generous dose of incredulity. I can't believe what other people obediently and passively believe.'

A lapsed, guilty, non-practicing Catholic, Dr Williams considered whether she should point out that faith provides some people with solace. However, she felt that might risk displaying her own values. Patients need to be kept at a distance and this was the beginning of a professional therapeutic relationship.

'Those are interesting thoughts Howard. What happened when you left the church signs and continued driving to work?'

'Not much. I drove straight to work and went to my office.'

'What do you do?'

'As I'm sure you are aware from the case notes I head the sales team for a car parts firm. At the moment. If they'll have me back after Friday's fun and games.'

Howard laughed softly and succinctly. 'Sales targets have been set at the same level as before the downturn and we're not meeting them. There's talk of redundancies.'

'Does that worry you?'

'No. I'm past caring.'

'Did anything unusual happen at work when you arrived?'

'Two things. The office was unusually quiet. Things have been a bit strained recently, but I got the impression I'd been the subject of comments immediately before I arrived.'

'How many people share your office?'

'Four. As head of the sales team I'm unpopular. It's my job to crack the whip.'

'Do you often get the impression you're being talked about?'

'No. Like I've said, paranoia is not my thing. It definitely went quiet.'

'What happened next?'

37

'I turned on my computer and, instead of the usual screen, something odd happened.'

Howard started to smile, laugh and maybe sob but it was hard to tell for sure. Dr Williams waited before asking him, gently, to continue when he was ready. Howard collected himself.

'The computer screen was blank except the words '0 *bootable partition in table*' were displayed across the top left hand corner.'

Dr Williams wondered briefly at the significance. The words didn't make much sense.

'What does that mean?' she asked.

'I don't know. The keys wouldn't work and I couldn't get rid of it. I turned the computer off and back on and the same thing happened. 0 *bootable partition in table* was there again in the same place. At first I didn't see it as a message, a sign, in itself, of anything. I saw it on one level simply as a glitch. I didn't think anyone had been messing with my computer either. However, I found it funny. It was a suitably absurd way to start the working day. Before I knew it I started to laugh and couldn't stop. My colleagues also laughed a little at first but, looking back, they were also concerned. My whole life led to this moment. 0 *bootable partition in table*. Every time I looked at that I laughed intensely. On one level, those words held the answers to the mysteries of the universe. Namely, that there are no answers. Here I was, an unhealthy, middle-aged divorcee at 9.03 on a winter's morning, in a soon to be redundant sales team at the back of an industrial estate and lo and behold this is what it all means. 0 *bootable partition in table*. I had found the truth. The meaning of life, the key to existence. It meant nothing and everything. The universe is both arbitrary and connected. I'd recently seen a t-shirt on a passing stranger that said "maybe the

Hokey Cokey *IS* what it's all about." It made sense, but it isn't easy to explain.'

At that point, Howard started to laugh again but his sobs were now easier to distinguish. Without prompting he continued. 'It's very hard to put into words what I was feeling. I felt free and powerful for the first time. I'd lost my chains. I could do anything. This was more of a feeling than a word thing capable of explanation.'

Dr Williams felt unsure about all this talk of meaning, absurdity and tables. She wanted to know a little bit about Howard's past, relationships, why he was estranged from his family. She felt things do matter, that we must try to be responsible for our actions and give them meaning. Little things matter even if we don't have an overall, bigger explanation for our lives. All of this would have to wait for next time because she had other patients. She thanked Howard for his time and made arrangements to speak to him again soon. Her hair was nearly dry. Mr Watson, the silent Staff Nurse, also thanked Howard.

Howard, in turn, thanked both doctor and nurse. He told Dr Williams he looked forward to speaking to her again, and, in time, to his diagnosis. He suggested she make it one he could be proud of. Nothing too trivial. In fact, he would, if she wished, self-diagnose. How about 'Generalised Existential Paralysis'? She could get it translated into French for maximum impact. His own French was poor but 'La existentielle paralysie generale' is about right. Jeffries Syndrome would also be suitable.

It was, after all, his condition.

Red Liquorice Laces

By mid-December my wife Sheila and I were at breaking point. She was hell bent on pestering me about affording Christmas presents for our children, Jane, nine, and Adam, eleven. I'd been made redundant from the washing machine factory in February and still hadn't found a job, just endless rejection and humiliation at being unable to continue providing for my family. A poor hunter. All sense of responsibility receded as I justified steadily slipping into habitual routines as tedious as the grind of the production line.

Sheila would get the kids up for school on the way to work and finish early to pick them up. I'd get up at noon, smoke in the back yard and wander down to the pub and join the regulars. Three or four of us always sat together and there were real characters to enjoy. I thought it would last forever. We all liked a good moan. Landlords, money and rent, our health, immigrants, the NHS, bad luck on horses, our lives. It was as if we were passive bystanders in life's circus, condemned to inaction. The world was wrong, it had let us down. I'd spent most of the redundancy and the bills were unpaid. By that December we were months behind on the rent and threatened with having the gas and electric cut off. Sheila's jobs, care worker during the week and counter assistant at a newsagent on Saturdays didn't pay enough.

On a Saturday I looked after the kids for Sheila while she went to work. I'd get up hung-over and start shouting at them. They'd make a noise, argue, play, ask questions and I couldn't stand it. Jane would look at me with condemnation and stick a few daggers in. She might ask, 'Daddy, where have you been all week? Where do you go? Is it true you drink lots of beer?'

'Who told you that?' I'd ask.

'Mummy.'

'I enjoy a drink with friends sweetheart.'

'Are you an alcifrolic? Aunty Joyce says you are. I heard her talking to Mummy.'

'No I'm not. Tell me what they said.'

'Just you drink too much and you're an alcif...'

'Alcoholic.'

Tired and sick I'd put an old Disney film on for the kids and fall in and out of sleep on the couch until mid-afternoon. Jane and Adam would watch some of the film, run outside, upstairs, and sneak off to a neighbour's house and go to the park. They weren't supposed to leave the house alone, but the deal was they could do what they liked as long as they didn't tell 'Mummy' I'd been sleeping. At around mid-afternoon I'd wake and fetch the kids from wherever they were. Feeling a bit better I'd usually take them to the Spar first where I'd buy red liquorice laces and a few packets of pickled onion flavoured monster munches. We'd sit on the park swings eating our goodies, lowering those laces into our open mouths before throwing some monster munches to the seagulls. On the mantelpiece there is a picture of the three of us chomping away. Sheila took the photo in happier times.

It's funny, but whenever we went to the park I'd feel happy to be with the kids. We'd talk about school, their friends, holidays, how they wanted to dress on Halloween, that sort of thing. The feeling never lasted though. I'd sneak a look at my watch and start resenting Sheila. It was her job to look after the kids. I'd done my bit and needed time for myself. Back home I'd put another film on and get ready to go out. At 5.30 Sheila would get home tired and start cleaning up the house and cooking tea.

It seemed fair to me back then. I deserved a few drinks. We would eat tea in silence. I'd kiss the kids goodbye, grab my coat and head off to meet the gang, leaving Sheila up to her elbows in dishes. No one could complain about my Saturday nights after a full day babysitting. On a Sunday I'd wake up mid-morning with a throbbing headache to the stale stink of armpits and sour booze. Sheila would be hoovering downstairs or chopping vegetables for lunch. The kids would be watching cartoons. I'd sway across the landing in my underwear with eyes half closed to make it to the bathroom before puking. After the first beery gush I'd wrap my arms around the porcelain underbelly of the toilet and remain for about twenty minutes retching. Sometimes I'd hear the kids saying 'Daddy's being sick again Mummy,' but Sheila would get on with her work. Adam liked to come upstairs and peer around the door and ask if we were still going swimming. I'd tell him 'Yes, son, but wait downstairs, I won't be long.' I'd take a slug of mouthwash, spit it down the loo, flush it all away and with foreboding heave last night's clothes back on.

No matter what the weather I'd walk to the baths wearing dark sunglasses. The queue would be long, the changing rooms full of loud excited kids. I'd keep those sunglasses on right up until I was ready to go into the pool and face the glaring lights. That entrance to the pool through the freezing cold footbath and into the noise sapped my spirit. The amount of time I spent in the pool with the kids became less and less until eventually I'd just let them go in on their own. They couldn't swim well so I'd tell them to stay in the shallows though they begged me to join them. I'd sit on the balcony with foam earplugs in and a plastic cup of vegetable soup from a vending machine.

Before leaving the baths I would wet my trunks under a cold tap and place them back within my folded towel so Sheila wouldn't know I hadn't gone in. Keeping Adam and Jane quiet was easy. If they promised not to tell we would stop and buy our favourite red liquorice laces and sit on the swings for a while before lunch. As the months wore on Sheila could barely look at me when we ate our sausages, mash and veg. I was out as soon as dinner was over, family duties complete.

Life followed a familiar pattern most of that year. Sheila and I started rowing more. One Sunday I woke, staggered across the landing and noticed the house was quiet. No vegetables being chopped, no kids shouting, no loud television. I went downstairs and found a note on the kitchen table from Sheila. She'd borrowed the train fare off her parents and taken the kids to stay with them in Liverpool over Christmas. She might even look for a new job and house up there. Don't bother to get in touch because she needed a break from 'us'.

I was thrilled. Not so much about the prospect of losing them all, but with the fact that I could have the day alone without going to the swimming pool. At that point nothing else mattered. After puking I went back to bed for an hour and slept soundly. I got to the pub an hour early that Sunday. Looking back, as soon as I walked in everything was different, more serious. One of the gang asked if I'd heard what had happened. There had been an enormous train accident. The 8.25 to Liverpool had derailed a matter of yards after leaving the station and the front half had plummeted down an embankment towards the beach below. I ran out of the pub towards the station, but it was closed off and filled with emergency service personnel whilst outside distraught locals and reporters jockeyed urgently for information. The embankment and beach area was also out of bounds. All I can remember is screaming at people about the kids and Sheila.

I tore home sobbing and frenzied. It was all my fault. They were leaving to get away from me and were now smashed up bloody and dead in the tangled wreckage of a train compartment. I turned on the radio. Exact numbers had not been established but the death toll was expected to be very high given the size of the embankment and the rolling of the battered carriages. A number for concerned relatives was given out. The sound of the front door key. In walked Sheila and the kids.

'Daddy, Daddy, there's been a train crash.'

Sheila set about dinner and explained that she had intended to get the next train to Liverpool at 9.25. She came back and took the kids swimming having found out about the accident. No need to cry, she said, avoiding eye contact, I could still go to the pub. Instead I took the kids for a walk along the estuary for the first time. They pleaded with me to buy some red liquorice laces on the way back but I explained that it's not good to eat sweets just before dinner. It spoils the appetite.

The Rings of the Lord

When I was a child I often stayed at my grandparents' bungalow in the countryside. It was a great place for a young lad to be, with chickens in the yard and a big wood at the back. One night when I was about fourteen my gran and I were watching a television programme about the afterlife whilst Granddad was busy in the shed making a model steam train. It was time for bed and I didn't want to go.

'Gran, do you believe in life after death?'

'Hmm. I believe something happens to us, that we go somewhere. It's a spirit world in another dimension with the Lord as guide and ruler. Some call it Heaven,' said Gran.

'There has to be proof in my view,' I said.

Gran looked at me thoughtfully for a moment. 'Do you remember me telling you I worked in a big old country house when I was very young, not much older than you?'

'Yes, the one with all the servants,' I said.

'That's right. Well, my mother gave me her diamond wedding ring before she died and I took it with me when I started work there. I'd put it on at night when I was on my own but didn't tell anyone about it or wear it when I was working. I kept it in the top drawer of the chest at the side of my bed.'

'So what's this got to do with the afterlife?' I asked.

'Be patient lad. One night I discovered it was missing and searched the room, turned it upside down.'

'Was it your own room or shared?'

'My own, just a tiny single room in the servants quarter. Anyway, I sobbed myself to sleep that night.'

The last bit caught my attention. Gran was lovely to me but she was a tough woman, deriding anyone overly sentimental as 'namby pamby'. She was much younger in her tale so I figured that maybe she just toughened up over the years.

'What happened next?' I asked.

'Well, I continued to look for the ring over the following week, thinking I might have left it on by mistake and that it may have slipped off somewhere. I knew this was unlikely as I had always been careful about returning it to the top drawer and it was a tight fit, something you would notice whilst scrubbing and cleaning.'

'Go on,' I implored.

'About a month or so later I was asleep but sensed a presence in my room. When I opened my eyes I saw my mother encased in light at the end of the bed.'

'Wow. That's amazing. I'll bet you were petrified Gran.'

'Not at all. I felt at ease but unable to speak. My mother silently beckoned me to get out of bed and follow her. I put on some night clothes and she led me through the maze of corridors and down the forbidden grand staircase.'

'Why was it forbidden?'

'In those days the grand staircase was strictly for the people who owned the house and their guests unless it was being cleaned and polished. Very strict. Anyway, we ended up in the kitchen where my mother guided me to the ring hidden behind some rarely used old crockery high up on a shelf.'

'Crockery?'

'Plates, cups and saucers, that kind of thing. Anyway, as soon as I saw the ring my mother disappeared. I turned around and she was gone. I placed the ring on my finger and crept back to my room using the servants back stairs.'

'So you got it back after all?'

'Well, when I woke up in the morning it wasn't on my finger or in the drawer so I was very confused. Later that

46

same morning I was working in the kitchen and I got the opportunity to look behind that old crockery and the ring was there so I slipped it into my apron pocket.'

'Your mother must have taken you to it in a dream otherwise she could have just given it to you. What happened to the ring?'

'Later that day I took it to my aunt and uncle's house as I was due a rare afternoon off. I've still got it. Do you want to see it?'

'Oh yes please. Maybe your mum knew you had some time off and chose that time on purpose so you could get it out of the house.'

Gran left the living room for a moment and came back with a small twinkly diamond ring, saying she still wore it occasionally when she felt the need and always on the date of her mother's death.

'Did you find out who took it?' I asked.

'No, but there was a housekeeper at the Old Hall who made my life a misery. I think it was her but I can't be sure. Do you want to hear another story or are you tired and ready for bed?' Gran said, with a glint in her eyes.

'Carry on Gran. You can't go up the wooden hill in a bungalow.'

'Straight to bed after this. Your mam would have my guts for garters if she knew what time you go to bed here. Ready?'

'All ears.'

'Many years later I fell ill and ended up in hospital with double pneumonia. I dreamt that I was walking slowly towards the top of a hill where dead relatives were reaching out to me.'

'The ones from those old black and white photo's wearing hats and waistcoats?

'Well, yes, at least the ones who were no longer around.'

'Did they manage to reach you?'

'I was about to grab one of the hands when the dream ended. The hand I reached for was my mother's and she seemed to be grasping for the ring on my finger. Your granddad had put it on me in the hope it would bring luck whilst I was in hospital.'

'What happened when the dream ended?'

'Well, when I woke up and, much later, able to talk, the doctors told me they were surprised I had pulled through against the usual expectations for someone so poorly. I don't think I'd have woken up again if I'd grasped one of those hands. I'd have been a goner.'

'Maybe it was just your mind playing tricks, Gran.'

'The Lord works in mysterious and mischievous ways young man. Time for bed. Pop out and say goodnight to Granddad and tell him to call it a night. He'd sleep in that shed if he could.'

'Can I talk to Mam about those stories?'

'Well, she knows about them but don't tell anyone else outside the family. People would think we're an odd bunch. Family secrets.'

'OK. Goodnight.'

When I crept to the shed to speak to Granddad I expected to find all those dead relatives in there. I didn't sleep that night. The woods at the back of the house seemed less than enchanted after all that talk and I thought I could hear breathing, far off laughter, and the snap of branches. I mentioned the stories to my mother but she seemed a bit annoyed that Gran might have frightened me so further discussion was not encouraged. I didn't know what to make of it. Even at that young age I didn't believe in anything supernatural. However, my gran was the most straight talking person I've ever known and certainly not given to flights of fancy. Indeed, her 'tell it as it is' approach riled many a family member over the years. I've often noticed

48

that my own dreams are always linked to reality such as a recurring thought, a snippet of seemingly inconsequential conversation, a deep seated fear, or something I've seen on television. I settled for the view that Gran had certainly told the truth but there was an explanation somehow in the way the mind makes sense of the unexplainable in a crisis.

Thirty years later, events in my own life served to deepen these mysteries through the most unlikely of sources. I watched a documentary about the golden age of British wrestling that activated a deluge of happy memories. My late granddad, who died a few years before Gran, used to sit on the edge of his seat at four o'clock on a Saturday afternoon ready for *World of Sport* and the wrestling on television. The documentary included footage of some of the wrestlers he loved and loathed such as Mick 'not the ears' McManus, Adrian Street, Johnny Kincaid and Jackie Pallo. Granddad used to yell at the screen, 'Pull his bloody ears off. He's a dirty beggar' or, 'He's a daft apeth just look at him.' After the wrestling, *Final Score* would come on with that monotonous screen and a dull voice reading the results. 'Heart of Midlothian 2, Queen of the South 1.' I'd be sat across the floor fascinated by those mysterious Scottish team names knowing that Granddad might creep up from behind and put me in a full Nelson until I submitted or Gran threatened to put him 'in the dog house' for messing about.

The one wrestler he loved and loathed more than any other was Kendo Nagasaki who had a move called the kamikaze roll that made Granddad wince every time he saw it. Kendo wore a leotard and a dark mask which no other wrestler was able to remove. It made him look really sinister, with holes for the eyes, nose and mouth and white horizontal lines that made his face look caged. He never spoke and neither did Granddad when Kendo wrestled, he just admired the action as if he was hypnotised.

49

The documentary had some great recent footage of a masked Kendo in his palatial house sitting in the background whilst his spiritual advocate spoke on behalf of 'the man behind the mask'. She said that in the 13th and 16th centuries the mask wearer had fought alongside the original Kendo Nagasaki as a samurai warrior and this had been discovered by past life regression. The man behind the mask is guided on this earthly plain by the ancient warrior. More down to earth commentators on the programme talked of how the myth surrounding the wrestler's lost half finger being cut off in a strange Japanese ceremony was, in fact, the result of a factory accident near his home in Wolverhampton, and that his real name was Peter. I thought it was hilarious but I think Granddad would have preferred the mystery. For a long time he thought Kendo was either Japanese or a member of the royal family. Gran said he wore the mask because he was signing on the dole and wrestling on the side.

Footage was also shown of the voluntary ceremonial unmasking of Kendo which I had watched avidly with Granddad just before Christmas 1977 and in more recent times on You Tube. It was at Wolverhampton Civic Hall. Kendo entered the barely lit arena masked and robed, with his manager 'Gorgeous George Gillette' and several acolytes. Gorgeous George told the crowd that Kendo had been to a secret retreat where he had built up his healing powers and the time had now come for his unmasking. Someone in the crowd shouted 'Rubbish' at this point. Kendo thrust his samurai sword into the canvas and knelt down with his robed acolytes at his feet. Salt was thrown over Kendo's head as the mask was slowly removed by Gorgeous George. When Kendo was revealed he had a shaven head with a bizarre occult like tattoo of interlocking triangles on his crown and the only hair was a long black ponytail. His eyes glimmered burning red as he faced the crowd silently, sword clasped in hands held high above his head in warrior pose whilst the mask was put on fire in a raised steel bowl behind him.

Some months after watching the documentary I had a serious accident on the motorway after dropping off Christmas presents for family members. I suffered internal injuries, concussion, fractures and burns. It was touch and go for the first week in hospital during which time I also endured a heart attack. My parents were told to expect the worst whilst they kept vigil night and day. When I eventually regained consciousness I was able to smile at them but unable to speak for another two weeks during which time I had a number of operations and treatments. My mother had inherited the ring and placed it loosely on my left little finger when the worst was feared, having asked the doctor's permission to do so. When I eventually started talking I was able to tell my parents about a dream I'd had.

I was at ringside watching the ceremonial unmasking of Kendo Nagasaki. Sitting with me were all the dead relatives that had reached out for Gran. They were in black and white, just like the photographs. My great grandmother wore the ring and my gran was there too shouting 'rubbish' when Gorgeous George was making the announcement. Kendo struck his sword into the canvas, acolytes at his feet, whilst Gorgeous George slowly lifted the mask. This time, instead of Kendo, my granddad was revealed with his bulbous nose, cauliflower ears and ruddy face without false teeth in. He had that same interlocked triangle tattoo, a ponytail, red eyes and a samurai sword clasped above his head. The spiritual advocate I'd seen on the documentary walked into the ring to make an announcement.

'Your granddad has summoned the spirit of the ancient

samurai warrior Kendo Nagasaki to channel a sacred message. "Don't die you daft apeth or you'll end up in the dog house with me".'

My bemused parents then told me that something very unusual had happened when I had been close to death. The doctor said that I seemed to be talking in an Asian language at times whilst unconscious. They asked a nurse of Asian origin if she could recognise it. She was unsure but thought it sounded Japanese. Another unusual thing was the date of my accident, 20th December. The same date as the unmasking of Kendo in 1977.

I've made a good recovery but I'm still not sure how I feel about all this. I'll be grappling with it for a long time to come. My mother has lent me the ring as she thinks I may need it but she insists on having it back occasionally. I often find myself gazing at it, checking it's in my drawer and wearing it whenever the craving takes hold. I've even considered telling my mother I've lost it so that I don't have to give it back but somehow I don't think the dead would let me get away with it.

Hide and Seek

When I was thirteen a beautiful nature reserve was opened by the RSPB alongside the estuary half a mile from town. It consisted of two large lagoons with small islands, reed beds, grassland and four bird hides. Sometimes at night my friends and I would hang out in the hides and smoke weed, drink cans of lager, snog girls, have a laugh. It was cosy in winter, though a bit spooky with the wind and cold. On the walls were pictures of birds with their names. Lots of ducks, herons, grebes, little egrets and more. We would take the piss, cup our fingers in the shape of binoculars, put on a boring, slow voice and say things like 'Oh yes look at this. A duck. Interesting indeed. And what's that over there floating past the reeds? I'm sure it's a Great Crested Grebe. So it is. Magnificent.'

Things got out of hand but we didn't care. Over the years we hurled wooden benches through the hide windows, ripped down the information boards, changed the names of all the birds to 'tit' or 'shag', sprayed 'Twitchers are pervs' on the walls, and glued the window latches. Locks didn't stop us.

The best night came on a Friday early one December. I was out with Jimmy, Billy, Steph, Liz and big Duncan. We were sixteen and in our last year at school. Our prospects were poor. Jimmy and Billy were brothers and their dad was in prison for GBH. They idolised him. Steph and Liz would do almost anything for a steady supply of fags. Big Duncan was violent. Mam tried to look after my two sisters and me, but was usually drunk by teatime. We were already ugly.

On the way home from a party we decided to visit the big hide that overlooked the estuary. It was past midnight when we got inside and the streetlights on the bridge nearby dimly lit the choppy water. We were all a bit pissed and noisy, taking turns to snog the girls, slurping lager, smoking, laughing, feeling alive. Big Duncan went outside and laid a giant shit on the shore especially for the twitchers. The two brothers silently rolled pungent joints, and the girls wrapped jackets around their cold chubby white thighs. I scorched the hairs and flesh of my arse with a gas lighter trying to ignite a fart.

Someone decided it would be a good idea to start a fire to keep warm so we put a couple of benches in the corner and set about burning them. We opened some windows to let out the smoke. Turning our backs on the fire we sat tight together in a row on the last remaining bench looking out to the estuary, sharing joints. Flames flickered and spat behind and the smell of burning wood reminded us of the town bonfire.

I was nearest to the fire and after about five minutes I could feel my back and hair getting hot. I turned and saw that the fire had caught the wooden wall of the hide and was licking, curling and spreading angrily. 'Fuck, the place is on fire,' I hollered and the others started yelling and panicking. We got out quick and the fire was visible outside with thick black smoke rising and drifting across the water. Big Duncan threw beer over the flames.

It was time to make a dash for the bridge where we could scamper up the side bank and get back across the main road and home. We were laughing breathlessly as we ran, clutching our beer, stopping for a quick chug, looking back as the fire grew and lit up the sky. Then we heard the sirens.

We got to the bridge, climbed the bank and hid in some bushes. The fire had completely engulfed the hide and we could hear it roaring and crackling like an enraged monster bursting out of the earth. It was a dazzling sight that illuminated the valley eerily, the houses across the estuary, the water, the lagoons and the reed beds. The wind moved and shaped the fire, centre of the universe. We watched the fire engines snake down a narrow path towards our inferno. They could only get so far and then the men had to pull thick yellow hoses attached like umbilical cords to the vehicles.

I took command. 'Right, none of you say a single word to anyone. One at a time get on to the road, cross for the footpath and head home. Remember we all walked home after the party and hung around the park a while. Act surprised when you hear about this. Sneak in if you can, go straight to bed and meet in Mag's café tomorrow at four. Duncan, you first.'

We listened for any cars and made our escape one by one. I was last and the police were on the scene by then. The bridge was made visible by the street lights and fire, so I walked across to the footpath as casually as possible, feeling exposed. My house was quiet. Mam was passed out on the sofa, empty bottles and a full ashtray on the cracked glass coffee table. I went straight to my room and slept in my clothes. At quarter to four the next day I set off to meet the gang. 'Don't be fuckin' late,' slurred Mam as I was leaving.

Mag's café was like a British version of a traditional American diner. A great hang out. Menacing framed pictures of punk bands like The Clash and The Sex Pistols adorned the walls. It was 1977. There was a colossal, thunderous jukebox in the corner with disco, punk, all sorts. 10p for two selections. I bought a lime milk shake, took it to an empty table and sat down.

Almost immediately the others drifted in, got their drinks and joined me. To make absolutely sure we wouldn't be overheard I put two loud punk records on. We cuddled close to talk. I did most of the speaking. We would meet here at Mag's every Wednesday at four to discuss developments

55

until the situation passed. They were to be called FOF meetings. Fellowship of the Fire. I'd invented a secret hand signal for members that involved putting one hand up with all fingers visible like flames and a simultaneous thumbs up with the other hand.

Over the following days speculation spread like, well, wild fire. A local arsonist had just got out of prison. People said he did it and that the police questioned him. Dead animals had been found and the fire had been started as part of a pagan religious sacrifice like in *The Wicker Man*. Irish gypsies from a site ten miles away were responsible. All kinds of rumours were circulating and it was the main topic of conversation at school on Monday.

Members of FOF took every opportunity to signal each other as we passed in the corridors or the yard. By the time we met on Wednesday at Mag's café the local paper was out. We'd been hoping for a front page headline like 'WHERE DO THEY HIDE?' and a large photograph of the fire at its peak, but had to be content with a short paragraph on page five and a Police spokesperson asking for info along with the usual condemnation regarding such mindless actions. Still, we loved feeling like fugitives. By the following week there had been a massive brawl between two feuding families in a village pub and another moral panic set in. We had one last meeting, kept up the signals and in a few months' time left school.

All that was nearly thirty years ago. The two brothers, Jimmy and Billy, were in and out of prison for years, but no one knows where they are now. Duncan trained as a long distance lorry driver and lives locally with his family. Liz manages a shoe shop. Steph is hardly recognisable. She became a junkie soon after leaving school. Her teeth turned nasty and fell out, her face shrunk and startled, body skeletal. I've been in and out of prison but I'm trying to go straight these days.

A year ago my probation officer, Colin, told me how he used to enjoy bird watching during weekends at the nature reserve when he lived near my village. He thought I should give it a try. I hadn't visited since the night of the fire, but one Sunday morning went along with some butties and a flask of tea. I took a pair of old binoculars and a book about British birds that belonged to my late Uncle Arthur. I headed for the place where the old hide had burned. It was rebuilt out of concrete blocks and a reinforced steel door.

I opened a small window upwards and latched it before adjusting the binoculars and opening the chapter on waders. Looking out to the estuary I saw some wonderful sights. The tide was quite far out and there was lots of activity on the mudflats. Small colonies of oystercatchers were wading near the water edge. I could make out their orange beaks, pink legs and gorgeous black and white plumage. Not far from them I came across four dull looking birds that had a kind of greyish brown colour. Not too impressed, I was about to look elsewhere when I noticed they had unusually long down-curved beaks. Looking through the drawings in Uncle Arthur's old book I identified them as curlews. Their long beak allows them to dig deep for lugworm and other treats.

The next bird I viewed seemed utterly prehistoric. Standing on a post near the shore was a large black bird with a long thick neck tilted to one side with its wings outstretched. I checked and identified a cormorant drying its wings. It was an amazing sight. Just as impressive was another large solitary bird standing on long legs with grey black and white plumage and a dagger like beak. It had a wispy crest at the back of its small head that made it look like an ageing hippy. This was a grey heron and it was the most elegant creature imaginable, Lord of the estuary.

I felt at peace listening to the distant bird calls echoing

across the mudflats. Since that day I've been to the reserve as often as I can. I sit in the hides overlooking the lagoons, eating sandwiches with a flask of tea, watching birds. I've joined the RSPB and have even trained as a volunteer. This involves demonstrating binoculars at the reserve shop, taking the public on guided tours, securing the hides and helping maintain the grounds. It gets me out of the bedsit, gives me purpose. One night a week I walk the reserve with a torch to check for trespassers and make sure the hides are locked. I caught a bunch of lads spraying graffiti on my old hide overlooking the estuary on one occasion. They scarpered double quick when they saw me coming.

Sometimes I let myself inside for half an hour or so before heading off. It's a sacred place. On the way home I nip into The Pied Bull in town for a pint. My old mates take the piss, but I don't care anymore. Occasionally I see Duncan having a quiet drink in the corner. We always greet each other the same way. One hand up with all fingers visible and a thumb-up with the other hand. FOF.

Peeling Away

Aunty Megan died whilst peeling spuds at the kitchen sink. Uncle Brian went into great detail about finding her. How he'd only nipped upstairs to use the toilet. How he'd come back to watch the second half of the match on television and could no longer hear her preparing dinner. How he'd called 'Megan' three times, each time louder, from his armchair. How he'd gone to the kitchen and found her with legs showing and purple pinny wrapped around her back. How he'd pulled down the hem of her skirt so she looked decent. How he performed resuscitation to no avail. How the ambulance crew tried to bring her back. How the funeral director took her body to the hospital morgue. How he'd found the sink half full of water with three peeled spuds and another half-finished on the draining board next to the peeler. How he'd sat and cried before ringing everyone up. How she'd meant everything to him. That Sunday when Aunty Megan died the whole family descended in dribs and drabs to her and Uncle Brian's house whose tale was soon soaked in cheap vodka and stout.

The place still hummed of roast beef when I arrived and all the dishes were piled up in the sink, including a pan with the remnants of mashed potatoes. Whilst washing up I overheard Uncle Brian in the hallway quietly asking my cousin Ronnie the final score of the match. Liverpool had won 2-0. 'Fantastic. Two more wins and the league is ours' enthused Uncle Brian before heading back to the living room, sombre.

Uncle John arrived genuinely shaken, offering condolences. He stood out from the rest of the family as a teetotaller with wry humour, good dress sense and carefully chosen words. He spoke of Aunty Megan's qualities, her selflessness, kindness, the perfect older sister, before joining me in the kitchen and picking up a tea towel. I asked when he had last seen Aunty Megan and it turned out they hadn't met up since her retirement party two years previously. 'You know how it is, you just lose touch,' he said.

Aunty Verity was next on the scene, sobbing and hugging as she always did at such times. She was one of Aunty Megan's two sisters, the other being my late mother. Breathlessly, she recounted the oft told story of how Megan, poor dear Megan, had looked after her brother and sisters when they were growing up whilst Grandma Sybil had been laid up for nearly a year with kidney problems. Granddad worked away a lot of the time so it was Megan who cleaned, cooked, shopped and everything else. All this and she'd have been barely fifteen. I glanced at Uncle Brian several times. Both eyebrows were raised incredulously, though a faint appreciative smile was also apparent. The two sisters hadn't spoken in years after a bitter row over Grandma Sybil's jewellery when she died, although Aunty Verity and Uncle Brian were notably at ease with each other.

Not to be outdone, Aunty Verity's daughter, my perfect cousin Susan, decided to offer her own tribute. We were treated to the story of how Aunty Megan, bless her, accompanied Susan on her first visit to the dentist as a frightened child. Her mean older brother, Andrew, had told her to expect the drill or a tooth yanked out on a piece of string attached to the door handle. It was Aunty Megan who held her hand and soothed her that day. And it was Aunty Megan who insisted on attending Susan's wedding whilst still recovering from her heart attack. Selfless, that was Aunty Megan, always thinking of others and putting herself last.

My cousin Andrew was very quiet. I went outside to the back yard for a cigarette and he joined me. He said he hoped the coroner would carry out a post-mortem. The way Uncle Brian treated her nothing would surprise him. Shortly after, I

60

decided to head home. I hadn't given much thought to Aunty Megan over the years. When I was a little girl, before my mother got a career underway, we'd visit her and Uncle Brian regularly. Aunty Megan was stern and would tell me off for anything, not saying please and thank you, being sulky, scruffy. I was usually referred to as 'she' or 'her' and it was only much later that I understood I'd been born out of wedlock and was therefore the embodiment of family shame.

My mother used to borrow a few pounds off Aunty Megan every now and then and would ask her for it fretfully in the kitchen before receiving a lengthy sermon about the need to manage money more carefully. I'd be sitting in the lounge with Uncle Brian who was always looking me up and down or putting me on his knee so that he could put his hands on my legs. His breath reeked of beer and he was sweaty. Best to visit when the football was on. He would then keep himself to himself other than the odd instruction for Aunty Megan to fetch him something from the kitchen.

When I got older my mother told me Aunty Megan made her siblings lives hell when she looked after them as kids. She bullied, harassed and swore at them daily. Interest was charged on the money borrowed to 'encourage thrift' during those lean times and mother didn't receive a visit from her when she was in hospital dying. Still, I promised my mother I would attend Aunty Megan's funeral one day as a mark of respect and appreciation.

There was no post-mortem and Aunty Megan was transferred to the Chapel of Rest. Most of the family went to see her. Apparently she looked peaceful. They'd done a good job on her at Wilson's the funeral directors. Got her hair just right and did her proud. I turned up at the service on my own, just on time, and sat at the back on one side away from most of the mourners. Aunty Verity was at the front, sniffling away into a handkerchief, mascara smeared over her face, looking around at the congregation before the service started. I noticed her back and shoulders jerking rhythmically to her sobs when it began. Uncle Brian, looking smart and shaven comforted her attentively.

Father McKenzie had been given some information about Aunty Megan and began the service by talking about her life. How she'd looked after her brothers and sisters, worked as a wages clerk in a soap factory, husband Brian and her had been inseparable. Always there for others, God would welcome such a giving person. As a Christian Megan Jones believed in eternal life with the almighty and had been chosen at this time to leave this world and join her saviour in the kingdom of Heaven.

A few hymns were sung about Angels, God's glory and repentance. Holy water was scattered across the coffin before the devout, starting with Uncle Brian, took part in Holy Communion. More prayers and then we were filing past statues of the Virgin Mary and heading towards the burial plot. Uncle Brian, Cousin Ronnie, Uncle John and Cousin Andrew carried the coffin and Father McKenzie said a few more words about everlasting life and how this marks a new chapter for Megan Jones.

There has been a long tradition in our family of putting letters onto the coffin of the deceased as it is being lowered into the earth or being taken away for cremation. As the coffin started descending Aunty Verity was the first to drop her letter in, followed by Uncle Brian and most of the other adults present. I'd thought about something to write the night before and made a few attempts, but I couldn't get the meaning right. In the end, I dropped in a folded blank piece of paper.

Some months later, I decided to visit Uncle Brian. Aunty Verity answered the door and I was served viscount biscuits and tea with a cup and saucer. It turned out that Aunty Verity had moved in to help Uncle Brian who, it must be said, was coping incredibly well. All that was ten years ago and I haven't seen them or any of the family since. I moved to the other end of the country to work at a university where I met Steve and we have a young son, Danny. It's funny, the only time I've ever thought about Aunty Megan and the others is when I've been peeling spuds. I've given the job to Steve now.

Picture This

I was lonely walking around the high street shops. It was early December and I hadn't had a girlfriend for two years. Or was it more? My bags were full of presents for nieces, nephews, brothers and parents, but I wanted to buy one for someone special. I should be that someone, a treat might lift my spirits. Late in the afternoon I came across a shop I hadn't noticed before that sold paintings and prints. It would be uplifting to find a picture for my living room as I had just moved into a new flat. There didn't seem to be anyone inside, despite the hordes scurrying in and around nearby shops.

The shop walls were sparsely and tastefully stocked with beautiful prints and a few framed originals so that each was allowed enough space to shine individually. Overhead lighting helped to make each picture a personal voyage. There was a golden Buddha, an old wooden jetty reaching out to a lake at sunset, a steam train hurtling through the countryside.

Most of the pictures appealed, but one encouraged a closer look. It was a photograph, from a slightly elevated position, of a lighthouse surrounded by an overwhelming swell of violent dark green waves so deep and high it was hard to imagine how the structure could withstand the ferocity. In the middle of the picture, just visible, stood a bearded lighthouse keeper in a yellow polar neck jumper looking out from the doorway. The waves were so angrily intimidating I felt like warning the keeper to get inside, close the door and head upstairs to avoid misfortune.

I stood for some time considering the image. It was carefully thought out so the viewer was drawn to the keeper, to feel the danger. Fanciful thoughts filled my mind about how the loneliness of the keeper in the midst of turbulence was a metaphor. I was a little startled when a chirpy, female voice to my left quietly observed, 'You're taken, aren't you?' Woken from my reverie I said, 'Yes I am' and was pleased to be in the company of a petite young woman about my own age. She had silently drawn up beside me and was admiring the painting too. Her name tag said 'Gwen' in arty calligraphy and she stood there in grey trousers, red pointy shoes, a yellow blouse and a black cardigan. She had jet black hair clipped short and punky on top of an unearthly pale face. With her hands clasped in front and her back straight she was in painting appreciation stance.

We both stood a few more seconds. At least that's how it seemed because I could only see a blur as I tried to decide whether I should conjure up some conversation. Maybe I should elaborate a bit about the painting, show her I'm the reflective, sensitive type.

'Are you local?' she asked.

'Kind of. I've just moved into a flat about five miles away. I'm always on the lookout for a new picture. Are you from around here?'

We faced each other.

'Yes' she replied, 'I live on the other side of town with my son.'

'How old is he?' I asked.

'Seven and he still believes in Santa Claus.'

'That's good. When he finds out Santa is really a credit card the magic will be lost. What's Santa bringing you this year?' I asked. It wasn't the gifts that interested me so much as who gave them to her.

'Shoes. I love shoes. My dad is getting me a new bike too. Hopefully some nice smellies as well. The usual. You?'

'I'd really like a new bike too, but Santa doesn't like me so I expect socks, aftershave...'

I was about to continue when an elderly couple walked in. Gwen abruptly excused herself and walked briskly back to the till. Relieved of her company I felt annoyed by the interruption and started walking slowly around, looking at but not seeing the pictures. Gwen was chatting to the elderly couple and I wondered what I could do to get talking to her again. For those few moments she had made me feel special. It had been some time since any woman had taken notice.

I couldn't resist the picture I had admired with Gwen. Casually, I stood behind the elderly couple at the till. They were surprised that a painting they'd come to collect hadn't arrived. Gwen was sweet and polite, reassuring them they would be contacted. She nipped around the counter and opened the door as they left.

'I've decided to buy the lighthouse print,' I informed her.

'Good choice. I'll nip in the back and get you a copy. Just a tick.'

When Gwen returned she carried an air of regret but no picture. 'I'm very sorry but we've run out of prints. The one on the wall is for display. Would you be able to wait until next week? We have one in our other shop in Chester. You can pay a deposit if you like to secure it.'

An odd way of doing business. And her manner was more formal. Still, I agreed, mindful that coming back to collect would give me an opportunity to see her again.

'OK. How much deposit?'

'How about half the price? Fifteen pounds.'

'OK.'

I gave her the cash and she wrote out a receipt. She asked for my contact details and said she would ring when the picture arrived. I thanked her, said goodbye and headed for the door. Again, she nipped round the counter and held the door open. Smiling, she said she looked forward to seeing me soon.

I looked forward to seeing her too. In fact I could barely think of anything else for the next week. I imagined the two of us falling in love over Christmas, playing snowballs, building a snowman with her son, proposing a champagne toast of togetherness for the New Year. However, nine days went by and I didn't hear from Gwen. I decided one lunch time to pop into the shop and make a casual enquiry as I did not have a phone number. I rehearsed a few lines on the way and looked smart hoping to make an impression.

When I arrived I couldn't believe what I saw. The shop was empty with a large sign stating: 'We are now closed due to unforeseen circumstances.' My first thought was that I would not see Gwen again. Next, however, I thought about the picture and my deposit. Surely Gwen would have contacted me if the shop was closing. I didn't know what to do, so I went back to work. That night I thought about the elderly couple and decided I should make enquiries the next day to the town council, citizen's advice and maybe even the police.

The following morning I sat down for breakfast with the local weekly paper. The front page ran the following headline:

Picture This – Shop disappears overnight!

Underneath there was a picture of the deserted shop and a story about how the people who were renting it had paid a month's rent up front and had only been open for about three weeks when they packed all their stock away in the middle of the night and disappeared without trace. Dozens of disappointed customers who had placed orders were furious.

'They ordered a print for me from their other shop in Chester, took a deposit and disappeared,' one customer stated.

The shop owners had given their tenants' details to the police, but these turned out to be false and the police were looking for further information and were keen to hear from anyone who had ordered items. The other shop in Chester did not exist. A number to call was included at the end of the article. The police came round and took a statement and the receipt. I never heard anything again about Gwen or my picture.

Ten years later I was on holiday in Cornwall with my wife, Joy. I saw that lighthouse picture in an art shop near a harbour and I mentioned to Joy that I loved it. When we got home a week later that wonderful picture was hanging in our living room above the fireplace. I looked at Joy and shook my head smiling. How she had managed to pull this one off was a mystery, but then she's full of the kind of surprises I like.

Brown Christmas

It's Christmas day. I'm twenty-two, sitting here in my bedsit by the sea.

It's the kind of place councillors are always bleating about in the local press. Houses of multiple occupation that attract ex-convicts, the unemployed and drug users. Apparently, ruthless buy-to-let landlords encourage some of them here by advertising dole by the sea in regional papers across the country. I'm an unemployed drug user. Heroin. Wrapped up in my little 'opiate cocoon' as the drug books say. I've got enough gear to last a week plus some to sell and I've stocked up with instant food too. Biscuits, crisps, tins of ravioli, instant mash, flapjacks. Not that I eat much anyway. If I need anything I can steal it. Nothing to worry about until New Year. I can just use, listen to music and take it easy like the bedsit zombie I am.

There's no one to bother me. Even the benefit office will keep off my back for a while about all those missed appointments and failure to attend interviews. My parents live across the country and they don't talk to me. Last year I broke into their nice semi to steal some money and jewellery but got caught by Dad whilst rifling through his and Mum's wardrobe. Dad rang the cops and we waited silently for them to arrive. I knew Dad better than to start sobbing and pleading. That would make me even more detestable in his eyes. He's ex-military. Charges were dropped eventually. My mum probably had something to do with that. So, no need to worry about seeing the family. They can keep their Quality Street, Marks and Spencer's deep filled mince pies and crappy James Bond repeats. The Queen can stick her speech up the corgi's backsides. None of it matters to me. Just gear and the rush that comes with a spiked vein. That's all.

Or so I thought. Last night, I started to let a few emotions back in. Wandering back home through town rekindled old feelings from the past at this time of year. I actually took notice of the decorations. Neon snowmen, Santa and holly in shop windows or strung along electric wires high above the streets, church bells ringing loud, the big Christmas tree and its lights in the town square, groups of town folk earnestly singing carols around it. Everyone wrapped up in hats, gloves and scarves. One part of me liked all that and another thought it twee. This town by the sea is much bigger than the village I grew up in with my sister and parents but it reminded me of that place last night.

Another thing happened on the way back to mine. I noticed the latest Rupert Bear annual prominently displayed in the local bookstore window. The eternally young bear looked as eager and happy as ever with his plain red jumper, yellow chequered scarf and matching trousers. I stood there for ten icy minutes gawping at that book. Forced myself to remember, to look back and recall a time when reading all those magical stories made Christmas that extra bit special. Every year I'd get two Rupert Bear annuals. One would be the latest and the other would be an old one tracked down by Dad. I thought about my parents and how they used to tell everyone about my love for Rupert. How they would catch me under the covers late on Christmas night with a torch reading about his adventures. I used to imagine I was really with Rupert and his pals in Nutwood. Rupert's deep sea adventure when he met King Neptune was my favourite. What a world to escape to.

Shop windows don't just display coveted items to tempt passers-by. They reflect the image of the window shopper too. I could see my image clearly last night, the windows offering a bright perspective due to the street lights and overhead illuminations. The purple tracksuit I always wear is a shocker. No style. No class. Black trainers nicked from Oxfam. My body is thin and pointy and cheekbones define my face. Then there are my teeth. Rotting away, falling out, deep yellow and brown, pink gums receding. It's easy to imagine how I'd look as a corpse in a chapel of rest. To think I was captain of the school rugby team and top in English Lit. I started to feel rough and, aching for a hit, headed off home.

Home is a first floor bedsit in the middle of the promenade. Walking up the burgundy threadbare carpet on the stairs last night I felt weary about the past and looked forward to nothingness. I opened the door, walked in and switched on a light. The place stank of old food, cold stale air and me. No decorations here except a couple of cards from customers on the floor and, by the sink, a saxophone playing Santa that I nicked from a Poundstretcher store. It lay on its back with the sax pointing to the ceiling.

Instead of settling in straight away to a night of oblivion I stood near the door and looked around. One room. At one end a small kitchen area that looks like it should be part of a 1970's lifestyle museum. Light green painted cupboards with plastic handles, stained Formica surfaces, dirty yellow ripped linoleum flooring and a rotting sash window with a soiled view of the fire escape. A large blue flip top bin overflows with empty beer cans and black streaked foil. The sink full of caked dishes.

I scrutinized the rest of this room I call home. On one side a torn mustard coloured two-seater sofa with foam sticking out of its arms and two legs missing. A low table heavily ringed with mug stains takes up the centre and a portable TV with a mini aerial occupies a corner on top of a spindly brown table with wonky screw off legs. A few feet from the TV is an old electric fire with a ripped plastic false coal flame effect with wooden shelves down the side which carry only dust. The walls themselves are a filthy cream nicotine colour and the carpet, which leads up to the linoleum, is grimy lime green. Things don't change much here, they just deteriorate. Walls get yellower and legs fall off the sofa.

Near the window overlooking the promenade I sleep on a small single mattress on the floor. It's damp over there and the wallpaper is bubbly. The old mattress is stained and smelly and sleeps like a hammock it's so knackered. My dark blue duvet cover, flung across sideways, has caught a damp pattern off the wall. The pillow has no case and no substance consisting of a mixture of blood, beer, fag burns and vomit stains. Close by is a small round metal waste paper bin. It's got a print of wild cattle like beasts going around it in the style of a cave painting. I pee in it at night because I can't be bothered to go out to the landing to the bathroom I share with the bloke upstairs. With the duvet around my shoulders I kneel, balance and then pee into the bin, moving the trickle and stream around, making a musical splashing sound that changes tone with the depth of urine. I then have a hit before going back to sleep, slopping out when I wake up. The first thing I see is the curtains. Faded dark green with a lighter spiral pattern and always, always closed.

I opened those old curtains last night. For the first time, I heaved the sash window upward and leaned out a bit. My stomach ached and I was sweating despite the cold. I could smell the salty sea. Street lights lit up the prom and I could see the dark rising of the waves beyond the metal sea barrier. They rose up closer and closer, the tops silver with the light, continually poised before crashing against the sea wall sending showers of spray and stones across the road. Over to the left stands a kiosk that sells ice cream, snacks and novelty gifts in better weather. I could just make out the daily special etched on a board inside a side window.

Tea or coffee with a buttered scone and jam for £2.50. To the right in the near distance stands a short decaying Victorian pier that looks as though it would go out to sea if the sea would have it.

Without warning, still half leaning out and looking at the waves, I felt tears on my face. I don't know why but the views reminded me of my old infants school and the crayon pictures of rainbows on the classroom walls. All the kids would sing 'Red and yellow and pink and green, orange and purple and blue. I can sing a rainbow, sing a rainbow, you can sing one too.' Light snow danced and pirouetted gently down from the heavens and a gathering of flakes itched my nose. Definitely time for a hit.

I walked over to my stash. Foil, lighters, syringes, straws, spoons, lemon juice, a bag of brown gear, skunk weed, king size Rizlas, filters, tobacco and a packet of Camel cigarettes all kept on a large metal TV dinner tray near my mattress. I picked it up carefully, sat on the old sofa and decided to chase the dragon. I placed a small amount of heroin inside a folded strip of tin foil and heated it up from underneath with the flame from a yellow lighter. The heroin turned black and wriggled around whilst I chased the fumes with a shortened straw. Within minutes I started to feel a warm glow in my stomach and then the kindness spread all over. Nice and dreamy and just content.

I smoked a cigarette. Usually, I smoke roll ups but I decided to smoke a Camel or two to celebrate Christmas this year. A treat. They were on special offer at Bargain Booze. I lit up and sent a cloud of smoke into the centre of my room. I watched it linger, almost blue, before it dispersed up down and sideways. No thoughts to bother me now. I just existed, smoking a cigarette. No deep and meaningful reflections, just inhale, exhale and watch. Doors slammed upstairs and I could just make out some raised voices but there was no need to pay any attention. I simply sat back with my eyes half closed and let time do as it will.

When I came round I had a great idea. In a cupboard there were a few old batteries so I fetched them along with the saxophone playing Santa. Before long I had old Santa on the coffee table churning out the tunes – 'Old King Wenceslas,' 'Rudolph the Red-Nosed Reindeer,' 'Silent Night.' His hips were swaying jerkily to the sound and his head nodded up and down with the sax at the same time. It was some show. Next, I turned on my CD player, plugged in the headphones and put some heavy dance music on. I just sat there watching Santa with the volume up high and I swear the old man from Lapland kept a perfect rhythm for every single track.

It's funny as hell watching Father Christmas straining away with so much enthusiasm to a fast dance tune and each time he stopped I picked him up and pressed the button at the back of his red cloak to start him off again. The cigarette smoke added a kind of Christmas jazzy atmosphere and I felt good about this world and my place in it. But those old batteries didn't last too long. I noticed that Santa started slowing down more and more until he ended up just swaying his hips every now and then before stopping in mid flow. I took off my headphones and pressed Santa's button a few times. He managed a quick shimmy and the final stalled notes to 'Silent Night'.

Time for a real hit. I cleaned up my abscessed left arm, boiled the kettle, let it cool, added a tiny amount of water to the junk on a teaspoon along with a little lemon juice to help it all dissolve, before warming it all up with a flickering flame underneath. Taking a new syringe out of its package I stirred the mix, placed a cigarette filter on the spoon and then sucked the junk up into the syringe before injecting a declining vein found by using my phone charger wire as a tourniquet.

Almost straight away I was overwhelmed by a rush. It felt like a worldwide climax that could only be resolved by death. I must have read that somewhere. But it was that good. My eyes closed and I leaned back into the sofa, staying in this dream state for some unknown time until suddenly brought back. On the coffee table Santa had burst into a swinging rendition of 'We wish you a Merry Christmas', dancing and playing like a dervish. It was nearly midnight. As far as I know Santa hadn't played that tune before. As soon as he finished the final note he stopped playing. It seemed like some sort of sign.

I've been thinking about last night. The decorations, the carol singing, Rupert, family, this bedsit, nursery school, the musical Santa. It's hard to make sense of it all but I can't go on like this. I'm going to get clean after the New Year. Start again. Contact the family. Get that Rupert annual in the sales. Detox. Methadone or Subutex. Rehab. Maybe even some work. Right now though I need a hit. I wish you a merry Christmas.

Signals

There isn't much privacy in flats. You know when people are washing clothes, watching television, hoovering, arguing, screwing, leaving, returning, smoking at the window, entertaining guests, drinking and sleeping. I rarely speak to my neighbours but I know their tastes, views, habits and routines. When I first moved in I barely picked up on all this beyond simply registering that this or that was occurring and getting on with my own life.

However, this year I've made a point of getting to know the Macpherson's better. Above my bedroom is their kitchen. I know this because at tea time, if I'm on the right shift, I stand on top of a step ladder to be close to the ceiling so I can hear what's going on. Pots clanging, tea's ready then they sit, eat and talk about the day. You get little snippets. The father, Jim, likes rugby league and isn't very strict. The kids wind him up and sometimes he chases them around roaring like a monster. The mother, Anwen, tolerates this kind of thing but likes to bring things to order particularly if the meal isn't finished. The kids, Warren and Rebecca, watch television in the living room whilst the parents clear up. I can hear the dishwasher sliding open and being turned on which cuts out the conversation. I do this from room to room. These days Saturday is *Strictly* night and on Sunday they all watch *I'm a celebrity*.

Lately, on a Friday evening, Anwen's sister, Sandra, visits for drinks and gossip, usually staying the night. Jim pops down the local and the kids go to their grandparents for a sleepover. I watch Sandra arrive if I'm home. Her car is a bit throaty and she parks up, slams the door and I get a glimpse of her walking hastily up the path to the front door. She's about thirty five or so, blonde in a bun, all flowing colour and jewellery. She has her own key and walks quickly up the stairs and along the landing past my flat, up to the Macpherson's place a bit more slowly and breathy. The door is already open as she walks into a hug and whoops of delight from Anwen. They spend a lot of time out on the balcony smoking, making it easy for me to hear them through my slightly open bathroom window. Three Fridays ago I heard the balcony door open so took my place in the dark listening intently.

'Well Sandra, have you and Robert decided where to go on holiday yet,' asked Anwen.

'Not yet. We're not getting on at the moment,' said Sandra.

'Don't tell me he's still working every hour he can.'

'It doesn't help but it's not that. I think I'm getting a bit bored of him. He never wants to do anything,' said Sandra.

'Jim's the same.'

'You love Jim though. It's obvious,' said Sandra.

'I do. Very much. And he's great with the kids. Why don't you do some things on your own if Robert isn't up to it?'

'Well, next Friday I won't be coming over because I'm off to The Crown Hotel for a meal with the girls from work. Ladies only.'

'The Crown's in the middle of nowhere. How are you going to get there and back?' asked Anwen.

'I'll get a return bus ticket. Last bus is about 11.30. Robert's working. Don't worry, I'll be fine.'

'Well if you get stuck ring us.' said Anwen. 'I'll keep off the wine in case you need a lift back.'

Sandra lowered her voice. 'Thanks. Does that weirdo still live downstairs?'

'Yes, not that we ever see him. It's always quiet down there,' said Anwen.

'I always get the odd feeling that he's listening to us,' said Sandra, even more quietly.

Both fag ends were flicked, still glowing, into the courtyard below as the two women headed back indoors. I checked my rota. The following Friday I was on the night shift until 11 and instead of driving to work I could get a return bus ticket and hopefully see Sandra. I work in an old rural signal box not far from The Crown and if my calculations were right, Sandra would get on two stops after mine. I knew from previous overheard conversations that she had recently moved to the area and lived on the other end of town to myself so would probably get off somewhere along the high street.

Other than catching the bus to work, the following Friday passed as normal. I swept the signal box, watered the flowers, cleaned the microwave, and kept the ledger book up to date. Passenger and freight trains passed through which I received and sent across my stretch of line. After work, torch in hand and rucksack on back, I took a short cut across the fields down to the main road and the bus stop. The bus came at 11.20 as expected. On board, a few people sat at the front so I headed for the back to be alone.

Two stops later, Sandra stumbled aboard. She nearly teetered back into the road whilst paying the driver before heading up the bus grabbing at hand rails and swaying around as the bus lurched forward. I thought she might give up but she kept on going, finally slumping at the back on the opposite side to me. She had dark smudged eye makeup, hair loose and long and she wore a flowing yellow dress with flat brown ankle boots. Quite lovely, her wrists were loaded with bracelets and her earrings looked like lightning bolts. Her dress was riding high and the low cut revealed awkwardly large breasts.

I looked out of the window or straight ahead pretending to be indifferent, glancing over discreetly at polite intervals. She started making retching noises with her handbag open, trying to puke into it but nothing came out.

78

'Sorry fella. I'm pissed,' she said.

'It's alright we've all done it,' I said.

She weighed me up, moving her face around like she was trying to keep the sick down and focus.

'That's not true. I'll bet you've never tried puking into a handbag before have you?'

'No but if you pass it over I'll have a go. Did you have a good night?'

'Not bad but I can hardly walk. I swear someone spiked my drinks.'

The bus started to slow down for a stop along the high street and Sandra got up to leave, straining to her feet, grasping for her bag. I joined her, moving swiftly in front walking slowly down the bus in case she needed a hand, turning to keep an eye on her. She kept missing the hand rails and half way down ended up falling and giggling into an empty seat next to a disgusted elderly man with a flat cap. She cheekily tilted the peak of his cap forwards and kissed him on the cheek. I offered her a hand and she pulled herself up keeping hold of my shoulders and rucksack until we reached the door where I helped her to the pavement.

We started walking in the same direction but I had to help her keep upright so she linked an arm with mine enthusiastically. I could smell a mixture of red wine and perfume from her face whilst her breasts danced along to a stumbling rhythm. She got chatty and told me she worked in the admin section of a parcel delivery service and had split up with her boyfriend that very day. I was asked over and over if I was a weirdo that preys on vulnerable women but I assured her this was not the case and that I simply wanted to get her home safe. She was convinced she'd had her drinks spiked and kept saying so, each time as if she was offering new information.

As we walked along I realised that she couldn't find her

place. We asked a few passers-by where her street was and after a few wrong turns found it. We said goodbye at the gate, she thanked me and I started wandering off, sorry the encounter had ended there.

I'd got about thirty yards down the quiet street when I heard the contents of Sandra's handbag crash across the pavement. She'd been reaching around for her keys and spilt the lot. I rushed back and found Sandra on her hands and knees trying to gather it all together. I could see her shape bent over and those milky breasts dangling and swaying in the dim light of the street. Together we put back her lipstick, phone, brush, hair clips, purse, tissues, mouth freshener, pens, diary, make up case and deodorant. In fact a whole world of insight into the life of Sandra, into the life of women. I'd never seen the full contents of a woman's handbag before. I picked up the keys and offered to open the door and Sandra agreed, inviting me in for coffee or wine. We struggled up two flights of stairs with thin purple carpet up to her flat and went inside.

I expected it to be messy because of the state Sandra was in but it looked a bit IKEA: tidy, bright and false. Laminated flooring everywhere. Sandra suggested I put some music on and get us both a drink so I chose a CD by *Ella Fitzgerald* hiding amongst the indie flotsam and NOW compilations before fetching a half bottle of red wine and two glasses from the kitchen. Sandra was in no state to hold the drink so I put it on the coffee table at her side. She was lying on her back across the leather sofa, her boots off and dress running very high. I could see her knickers, dark and smooth and those breasts wobbling slightly as she breathed. She focused and invited me to sit down at the other end of the sofa, instinctively reaching out to cover her legs at the same time.

'What the fuck have you put on? Who's this?' she asked.

'*Ella Fitzgerald.* It's pretty quiet. I was thinking of your neighbours.'

'What's your name again?'

'Chris.' I'd already told her many times.

'I swear someone spiked my drinks. I'm so pissed. I feel like I've been drugged.'

'Maybe you just had too much to drink. You should go to bed and sleep it off,' I said.

'Don't get any ideas.'

'I'm not like that. You're too drunk anyway,' I said.

Sandra seemed to be drifting to the music and soon her eyes shut and head nodded. She started snoring in a gentle, feminine way so I turned the music off and waited until she was out of it. I located the bedroom, opened the door, removed a wash bag and some clothes off the bed and folded the duvet over to one side before going back to scoop her up. She barely stirred as I laid her down stinking as she was with the wine and the perfume mixed together all sour. I put the duvet back across and manoeuvred her gently into a sideways position in case she was sick.

Back in the living room I fell asleep. It was one of those heavy naps and I woke up disorientated. With rucksack over a shoulder I tip-toed to the front door. On a shelf was some unopened mail so I made a mental note of Sandra's second name, closed the door stealthily behind and ghosted down the stairs out of the building. With a few more wrong turns on the way I got back to the high street and headed home for sleep but I couldn't stop thinking of Sandra and the way she linked my arm when we got off the bus.

The following week I made a few enquiries by ringing the parcel delivery companies asking for Sandra, using her second name. The third call was successful. The woman who answered said she would put me through. I put the phone down and headed to the parcel depot later in the day and sat in my car where I could see the staff coming and going. I saw Sandra walk out of the offices at the side and head for her car. I decided to follow her home.

She stopped at Asda on the way and I needed a few things so it was quite handy. Sandra bought apples, potatoes, decaf coffee, a tin of stewing steak and a loaf of wholemeal bread. Sliced. I followed at some distance and stood behind her at the checkout. She placed a divider between our shopping and I thanked her and was rewarded with eye contact and an inviting smile. She'd gone by the time I got out but I used the sat nav to get to her street where I saw her heaving the shopping through the front door as I drove past.

I continued thinking about Sandra most of the time that week. She'd taken a bit of a shine to me, I was sure of that. Otherwise she wouldn't have invited me in. Single now, she'd be available too and that smile between us at the supermarket lingered longer than necessary. I imagined us together, going to nice places, walking through the park hand in hand, cinema, and holidays. As expected, she turned up at the Macpherson's on the following Friday. I watched her arrive as usual through the gap in the curtains and stood near my front door to hear her breathy landing and stair climb, the whoops of delight. Soon she was outside on the balcony with Anwen and I was ready in the bathroom, crouched under the open window.

'How did your night at The Crown go last week? I was going to ring you but fell asleep,' said Anwen.

'I was so pissed I could hardly walk. I'm sure someone spiked my drinks,' said Sandra.

'Did you get the bus home?' asked Anwen.

'Yeah, the last one. Some weird bloke walked me home.'

'Bloody hell that's dangerous Sandra. You're lucky he wasn't some kind of nutter.'

'I can barely remember any of it. He ended up in the flat too,' said Sandra.

'Oh. My. God. You should have rung me. You were drunk, you may have had your drinks spiked and you let a complete stranger into your flat. That's madness Sandra.'

'I know. I don't think he did anything though. He'd gone by the time I woke up.'

'Who was he? What did he look like?' asked Anwen.

'I can barely remember. I think he had dark hair and a moustache. I've no idea who he was but he seemed friendly and concerned to get me home safe as far as I remember,' said Sandra.

'I'll bet he was. Next time ring me or you'll end up being a statistic. The world is full of weirdos,' said Anwen, lowering her voice. 'Imagine if it was that bloke downstairs. He's got dark hair and a moustache. Anything could have happened. The kids saw him a few days ago on the stairs. He asked them how they are getting on at school.'

'Don't Anwen, it doesn't bear thinking about. By the way, the flat below mine will be empty at the end of the month. The landlord asked if I know anyone who might be interested. I don't but if you do, let me know,' said Sandra.

'I don't to be honest. Why doesn't he put it in the Gazette?' asked Anwen.

'He has but asked me to let him know if I knew someone anyway,' said Sandra.

The lit fag ends passed my window. Sandra and Anwen settled in to a night of wine, Motown, laughter and the departure of Robert. I watched Sandra leave the next day at 10am, and then I nipped down to the newsagents for a Gazette.

The Cup Final

In '87 our village pub football team, Red Dragon Rovers, improbably reached the Webster Paint Sunday league cup final. The location was the ground of our hated local rivals from the next village whose team were called Merlin Athletic. Each year a team took turns to host the final. To add spice to this encounter, Merlin Athletic were the other finalists. They had already easily secured the league championship without losing a single game all season. They had beaten us in two ugly games already in the league, 0-2 at our ground and 3-1 at theirs. We ended mid-table in a league of twelve, which wasn't too bad for us.

Playing the cup final against Merlin Athletic at their ground was daunting. They had a great team by Sunday league standards and a hostile crowd backing them wherever they went. There had been violent tackles in the previous games between us; three players sent off and fan scuffles. I was anxious during the build-up. If ordinary league games could provoke such hostility then a cup final would be a bloodbath. My nature was and remains placid and I didn't enjoy the brutality that typified Sunday football. I'd been spat at, punched, head butted, called every name except my own and kicked around cold and muddy football pitches for five seasons. On my Monday postal round I'd be sore.

I vowed the cup final would be my last game and I would stick to playing five a side with friends thereafter. Besides, I'd promised as much to my girlfriend, Rhiannon, who refused to watch me play after a nasty incident at a game she attended. We'd been together for ten years and had started going out in school. I was ready to settle with her. I'd had a good final season though. From midfield I'd scored ten goals and won six 'man of the match' awards voted on my behalf by opposing managers. I was good at splitting defences with long-range passes into space for our forwards. Good vision.

We'd had a relatively easy run to the final. However, the semi-final had been a tough one against the third placed team in the league, Druids United. We scraped past them on penalties after a 0-0 bruiser and extra time. I scored our first penalty but the Druids' 'keeper took their last one and it sailed over leaving our winger, Gwynfor 'the human greyhound' with the task of hitting the roof of their net. He did and we piled on top of him and celebrated at The 'Dragon until dawn. Even the expected news that Merlin Athletic had hammered Griffin Wanderers in the other semi-final didn't hold us back.

The following week we started training. Our Manager and coach, Ifor 'the coal', put us through our paces. Training was now three times a week until the final in two weeks' time. Ifor was an ex-miner with a tough reputation and a nasty cough. He had us running up hills, doing press ups for slacking, skipping, shooting practise, tactics, team talks about the opposition, advice on how to foul without getting caught, how to go down when fouled, intimidation. Nothing was left to chance. Ifor said he rated us, that at our best he knew we could beat Merlin Athletic. He had seen weaknesses in their side. We must play the game of our lives and believe in ourselves. It was his last season and he wanted this 'if it's the last thing I do'. Besides, his smug brother-in-law, Gavin 'the scab', was his opposite number over at Merlin Athletic. Gavin and Ifor had worked down the pit as close colleagues and friends until the miners' strike. Ifor stayed on strike but Gavin crossed the picket line and went back to work. There had been no spoken contact between the families since and the two managers did not shake hands before or after the league games. There was no place in our team for anyone with any connection to the wrong side of the strike.

Training sessions helped focus body and mind. The team promised not to drink for a week before the final. Smokers vowed to cut down in the build-up. There was a togetherness we hadn't had all season. Pete 'the shank', our long yet portly centre forward, persuaded his boss at the local butchers to sponsor us for new cup final jerseys, which would be unveiled by Pete on the day. Gwyn 'the fish', our left back, offered the team free fish and chips at his dad's chippy in the village after the game if we won. A small gesture, but significant.

Anywhere in town we went, good luck was passed our way. Merlin Athletic were despised. For years rumours had been circling about interbreeding in their village, perverts, occult rituals and anything else that could make the place contemptible. Bragging rights were at stake and the pressure overwhelming. The week before the game I woke up more nervous each and every morning. Rhiannon and I niggled each other though my irritability was the cause. Nothing else was talked about and I posted a few letters in the wrong houses for the first time in years.

One thing that made it even worse was that the player I would be marking, Ginger 'the beast' Hughes, was an accomplished brawler who had been inside. A brutal murder had occurred recently in the woods behind our opponents' village and most of our players thought that Ginger could well have done it because the murdered chap had been out with his sister at some point. The last time we'd played he got sent off for scything away relentlessly at my ankles. I was on my back looking up, holding my left ankle in agony when he was given his marching orders, swearing and snarling that he would give me worse next time. I believed him.

The Saturday night before the Sunday final we went to Ifor 'the coal's' terraced house for homemade pasties courtesy of his marvellous wife, Ffion. We called her Aunty

Ffion and she made the best gravy. Pasty, mushy peas and gravy followed by some of Ifor's home grown rhubarb with lashings of thick custard. We crammed into the living room to play dominoes, talk tactics and just be together. It was Ifor's way of keeping an eye on us.

Some of the lads asked how I felt about playing against 'the beast' again when he was rumoured to have been in more trouble for GBH outside a nightclub in the city. I made light of it by saying that I'd heard he was scared half to death himself at the prospect of facing me, but the mirth that greeted my comment made it seem even more unlikely. The murder rumour resurfaced with gory detail and Ifor told us one of their player's brother was a policeman who had waved money, known at the time as 'Scargill's notes' at the picketing miners. He wouldn't tell us which player.

Aunty Ffion made her views on the match clear. 'I hope that brother of mine gets his comeuppance, the sly bastard.' She refused to come to the game. 'I won't share breathing space with a scab,' she insisted.

I couldn't sleep that night. We met on the big day at noon at our own pitch for a light training session and ham sandwiches courtesy of Aunty Ffion. Much of the time was spent talking tactics again. Ifor wanted us to play a sweeper system and forget trying to catch Merlin Athletic's quick team offside. We had been working on this aspect in training. Our centre half and captain, Dewi 'the bins', was to play deep in our defence to mop up any attacks that broke through. Dewi was overweight, 35, with a beery red face, but he was deceptively fast with plenty of stamina. In training he had mastered the role and his timing in the tackle was immaculate if overenthusiastic. He wasn't a fancy player; he did his job and laid the ball off to the creative players. The Nobby Stiles of the team. We needed him to be on top form. Our goalkeeper, Elfed 'the vampire', was a bit scared of crosses so our tall forwards, Pete 'the shank' and Dafydd 'the milk' were to come back for each corner to help snuff out the aerial threat. My job was to feed the forwards and calm the midfield. Ifor also instructed me to 'go down sharpish if 'the beast' tried his tricks.'

At two o'clock we piled into the cars and headed in convoy to Merlin Athletic's pitch. It was an overcast mid-May day, and I drove Rhiannon's second hand red Ford Escort to the ground, picking up three others on the way. There was already a crowd of about fifty of our supporters cheering when we got out of the cars before heading for the small changing rooms, a converted cow shed, at the side of the pitch. Merlin Athletic were already on the field in matching club tracksuits looking organised. I noticed 'the beast' and our eyes met briefly. He made a quick cutting motion with a finger across his neck before turning away nonchalantly. I headed for the toilet.

Whilst in the loo I heard raucous laughter from the lads. I soon found out why. Pete 'the shank' had unveiled our cup final jerseys. They were our usual colour, blue, but with a black cow logo hand sewn onto the right of the chest and 'Jones and sons butchers' written in black marker pen underneath. On the back, the numbers were not quite straight and sown on with big stitches and on each left arm the words 'Webster's cup final 1987' were written in that same marker pen style. Worse was to come. Each jersey was the same size, a job lot. Pete 'the shank' and Dewi 'the bins' couldn't get the jerseys completely over their bellies so they looked even less athletic than usual. Ifor was furious and wanted to head back for the old kit, but there wasn't time. Only Elfed 'the vampire', our keeper, got away with it as he had brought his own jersey. What a sight we were trotting out to the pitch. Merlin Athletic's players were laughing along with their crowd. They looked smart and their warm up routine well-rehearsed.

Before the game our team took it in turns to kick the occasional ball at our 'keeper or spread out stretching individually. Ifor got us into a big group hug and gave us our final, familiar instructions. Take no shit. Go down if they start hacking, forget offside, any chance you get, shoot, if in doubt kick it out, forwards: back for corners. Dewi 'the bins' was not allowed past the half way line. We could do it, it was his last season, he believed in us. The referee blew his whistle for the captains to gather at the centre circle. Dewi walked up with his short top and belly on show to shake the slim Merlin Athletic Captain's hand. It seemed a harbinger. A coin was flipped, Merlin Athletic won the toss and the game kicked off.

That first half Ginger 'the beast' Hughes continually backed into me, using his elbows when the ball was nowhere near, threatening to break my legs and put my lights out. I didn't say anything, didn't dare, but I won every tackle and challenge in that first half and gave as good as I got. The real stars were Dewi 'the bins' and Elfed 'the vampire.' Dewi mopped up everything with such authority he instilled a steely confidence in the team. His tackles were statements. On one occasion towards the end of the half 'the beast' was on the receiving end of a challenge by Dewi that was so rugged and complete in its timely execution it defined our resilience. It wasn't a foul, but 'the beast' was shaken and claiming he'd been upended. The referee waved play on and Ginger and Dewi exchanged hostile words. Just another incident, but pivotal. Ginger became a little less bullish.

Elfed was kept busy with crosses that he plucked from the air anywhere in his box giving the team further confidence. He made a fantastic save from a long range shot that dipped through the air towards the top right corner of his goal. We soaked up pressure that first half without giving away many chances. Our forwards barely got a kick. Their crowd called us all sorts. I was a bald bastard. Dewi a fat twat. Chris, our right back, was Pinocchio. Still, it was 0-0 at half time, we were still in with a shout and used to name calling. We did it to ourselves. Self-depreciating humour was part of the Dragon's team spirit.

As we sucked on our half oranges at the break and sponged down a few bruises, Ifor, wheezing and rattling, told us Merlin Athletic looked shaken when the half time whistle blew. He was probably right. They were frustrated towards the end of the half and had started to torment each other. Before we went out again Ifor suggested we visualise lifting the cup as victors and told us to keep our shape. Those ridiculous cow patches were half hanging off most of the players and so were the numbers on the back. Still, we had got to half time without conceding a goal and those scruffy shirts just added to our David and Goliath mentality.

Out we trotted for the second half to the sound of cheers from our supporters. It was a dismal game. We had a couple of half chances and Merlin Athletic had a genuine penalty appeal turned down. Otherwise it was long balls booted high up the pitch, bad tackles, verbal insults, bookings and increasingly nasty referee bating from both sets of supporters each time a decision went against their team. The atmosphere was heavy. The clouds were darkening and early on in the half there was torrential rain which smudged the marker pen writing leaving big blobs of black over our chests and arms. I was being singled out for real abuse from the supporters due to my baldness and responded with a few crafty hand signals when the referee and linesman wasn't looking. That only made it worse. There were boos every time I went near the ball and any move I made close to the side where those supporters stood was met with loud hostility, jeers and threats.

A few of our supporters started chanting 'scab, scab' in return, though Ifor oddly put a stop to that. I started to play with increased confidence the more I was berated.

With five minutes to go we won a corner. Gwynfor 'the human greyhound' floated one in for the forwards, but the ball was cleared by a Merlin Athletic boot long and high over all the players towards the centre circle where I was standing alone. The ball was bouncing when it arrived at my feet so I decided to play to the crowd a bit. I flicked the ball and kept it up about three times before passing it from thigh to thigh. Then I started heading it. It was surreal. Our crowd and players were screaming at me to pass it or do something and someone in their crowd pleaded 'Kill the bald twat.' Dewi 'the bins' was about twenty yards behind me and he screamed at me to 'watch out.'

While I was heading it I glimpsed Ginger Hughes tearing towards me, imploring 'I'm going to put your fuckin' lights out.' Just as he was about to take a leg breaking lunge I brought the ball down and volleyed it high and forward. I didn't see where it went as I was too busy jumping away from the beast. I avoided him by swiftly hopping to the side and throwing myself to the ground. Before I got up our crowd cheered and whooped hysterically and all the lads were bounding my way with manic expressions of disbelief and utter delight. I'd scored a beauty!

I was at the bottom of all those ink stained muddy shirts and flesh. When I eventually emerged, glad for breath, Ifor was gasping orders at us to keep our shape for the time left to play. Merlin Athletic threw everything at us. Ginger was like a bear with a full set of bad teeth. He promised he was going to kill me and within two minutes of the restart was sent off for trying. He literally kung fu kicked me when we went in for a challenge and left me in a heap on the floor holding my side in agony. Both teams were pushing and

91

arguing and our lads were straight in the mix. I was proud of them for that. Dewi was having a right go at Ginger as he left the pitch with supporters of both sides war ready. Some even came onto the pitch. It didn't matter. There was no time left for Merlin Athletic and the final whistle came soon after the game restarted. Ifor staggered onto the pitch with his arms in the air and all our supporters and players flooded towards me. I was thrown in the air, kissed, praised, made to feel like a God. There was more to come.

The cup had been brought onto the middle of the pitch and placed on a trestle table with the medals and another small cup. A local councillor with a microphone beckoned everyone to gather around the centre circle. He congratulated the teams for their performances and started the announcements. Firstly, the 'player of the year' needed to be declared as it had been won by a player from one of the teams. Dylan Williams had been outstanding all season, scoring goals from midfield, a model of consistency and had now scored the winning goal in the cup final. A big hand for Dylan, 'Webster paint Sunday league player of the season'. I went to pick up the small trophy and, to my surprise, now things had calmed, even the Merlin Athletic fans applauded, slowly at first. Our opponents picked up their losers medals to loud cheers and we collected our winners' medals. The councillor asked the Red Dragon Rovers Captain to come up and receive the trophy. Dewi 'the bins' slapped me on the back and told me to go and get the cup. He said I deserved to, this was my day. I walked up to the shiny cup, kissed it and lifted it above my head like the players on television. When I brought the cup down I could see my happy face reflected in it. Next thing I knew I was lifted again into the air and the whole team and our supporters paraded me around the centre of the pitch. I knew then that no feeling could ever compare, the moment had to be treasured as sacred.

From that elevated position I briefly caught sight of Ifor

'the coal' on the side of the pitch coughing his guts up with hands on knees and head between legs. Gavin 'the scab' wandered over to him to offer his hand and a few words, but Ifor drew his hand in and turned his back. Team pictures were taken by the local press and some supporters before we headed back to the changing rooms where the celebrations continued.

The wall between the two teams was thin and we heard a few threats and insults come our way, but nothing could stop us. We sang louder, sprayed champagne, drank from the cup and lifted Ifor in the air before drenching him in the showers. He didn't care. The tough old boy was openly crying with sheer joy, but he went straight home after. Still, we got into the cars and headed for Gwyn 'the fish' dad's chippy for our free slap up dinner. My car had the cup, held outside the passenger window all the way back to our village for passers-by to admire. We bundled into the chippy parading the cup and took full advantage. Gwyn's dad joined the party. We could have anything we wanted. I can still remember what I had. Steak and kidney pudding, chips, peas, gravy, two bread and butter and a mug of tea. I got that under my belt in no time and then we all headed to The 'Dragon for a wild celebration.

Rhiannon was there waiting and I hushed the pub, went down on bended knee and proposed. She accepted and when we had a quiet moment she informed me that the timing of the proposal was perfect as she was pregnant and a proposal before I knew felt so much better. I've never drunk that much since. Everyone wanted to buy me a drink and I was hoisted into the air at the end of the night in the streets and carried home legless in the early hours. The following evening I went to see Ifor 'the coal' and Aunty Ffion. Between them they told me that Ifor had the coal miners' disease black lung and did not have long left. The cup final had given him revenge over Gavin and he would die happy now. He made it clear that there were certain people who should not attend his funeral even over his dead body, and a week later he passed. We gave him a hell of a send -off. The coffin was delivered to the crematorium in an old coal wagon. Coal killed Ifor but the pit had been his life. The church was crammed with ex-miners and their families. All the lads kept their eyes on Aunty Ffion after Ifor died, but she only lasted a year. She got a similar send off and her role during the miners' strike, marching, organising collections and benefits, helping to run a soup kitchen, were emphasised in the sermon. I didn't play Sunday league again, I retired at the top.

That goal still gets talked about in our village. The locals, even the youngsters, still talk to me about 'the greatest goal ever scored', embellishing the story so the quality of the goal improves with each telling. One version had me on the penalty spot in our own half when I scored. Many a pint of beer has been bought for me at The 'Dragon and the old timers still give me a holy bow, arms above the head style, when I walk in on a Saturday night. There's a special section in the bar, overlooking the pool tables, where there are cup final day framed photographs of me holding the cup, carried by the other players. Also framed, but now yellowing, is the local paper headline; 'Pete the post delivers a miracle' with two pictures of myself next to each other. In one I'm wearing my football kit and in the other my postman uniform.

So much has happened since. Rhiannon and I divorced after bringing up three children. I became a manager with the post office and soon I'll be a grandfather. The goal has followed me through the years. When I was going through my divorce the goal seemed like a weight on my shoulders. I felt such a failure and wondered if I would ever achieve anything like it again. Many times I wondered if that day was the pinnacle of my life, the one moment I transcended my limitations and produced something memorable. I've never achieved anything comparable, other than my kids. At other times, when lacking confidence, I've looked back on the goal to give myself a boost only to remind myself I didn't even try to score; I just booted the ball up the pitch in panic. Still, it's nice to be remembered, and a spectacular fluke goal in a Sunday league cup final will do for me. A week never goes by when I don't think of that day, that goal, the player of the year award, the proposal, the celebrations, the euphoria of life and its possibilities.

Not long ago I was in a country pub at a wedding, standing at the bar hugging a pint. A big man I barely recognised came up, shook my hand and insisted on buying me a drink. He told me I had scored the best goal anyone had ever scored and he was the closest person to me when I scored it. It was Ginger 'the beast' Hughes and a more polite, funny man I've yet to meet. These days I call him 'Kung Fu Bambi'. I told him we thought he was a murderer back in the day and he surprised me by saying their lads thought I'd done it. He introduced me to his sister, Valerie, and we are getting married in the summer. Ginger is going to be best man and I already know what some of his speech will be about. The goal lives on.

The Day Before

Mark Farley woke to his 6.15 radio alarm and a reporter lamenting Iraqi atrocities. For some this would be a punitive emergence from slumber, but Mark found it preferable to startling music. Current affairs energised. Reaching for the clock with half open eyes he cut off the news using the illuminated digital numbers as a guide to the snooze button. His left arm and shoulder felt the cold so he pulled the duvet close and squeezed his lids tight before kicking the cooled hot-water bottle off the end of the bed.

The news came on again. This time there was talk of the title race between Chelsea and Manchester United. The English cricket team had finally won a match and Mike Tyson was undergoing drug rehab. It was 6.20, time to reach for the bedside lamp. With eyes still shut he knew just how high to lift and angle his arm before placing his fingers under the shade and onto the switch. Gradually opening heavy lids, he peered at his clothes, neatly folded on top of the chest of drawers, dark blue socks placed together in a ball on top as usual.

At 6.25 Mark raised his upper body and swivelled so his feet went straight to the floor. He always slept naked but felt the cold sharply, so he launched himself towards his clothes. The news had become the weather. Dark clouds and rain in the morning giving way to possible winter sunshine by mid-afternoon and then more rain at tea time.

After turning off both radio alarm and lamp, Mark wandered downstairs to the kitchen. The choice of breakfast cereals had been troubling him since the night before. He liked each equally. Weetabix, Frosties, Crunchy Crisp or porridge. In the end he chose porridge because it would be warm and filling. After breakfast he made a mug of strong tea and sat in the living room to contemplate the day ahead for ten minutes without too much noise.

He checked his watch. It was nearly ten to seven, as expected. He used the bathroom, brushed his teeth and headed for the hallway where he kept his little black mynah bird, Adolf, in a large cage. Leaning in, he puckered his lips and said, in a baby voice, 'Daddy loves you. See you tonight.' Adolf called him a 'cheeky bugger' and Mark turned around, carefully took his long black winter coat off the stand and heaved it on.

As he stepped outside a plastic bag swirled by, gathering speed with the wind before disappearing around a corner. The breeze was cold and harsh so he walked quickly, hands deep in coat pockets. The seagulls acknowledged his presence with hectic cries and the usual two people stood waiting for the 7.10 bus into town; an attractive woman in her mid-thirties Mark recognised from school and a man in his late fifties who always smoked and avoided eye contact. The woman also ignored Mark and turned away slightly.

When the bus arrived the smoker flicked the last third of his cigarette into the street. The passengers boarded by the unwritten code of arrival; the smoker, the woman, Mark. After paying Mark slumped near the window at the rear. The journey took twenty minutes. Images of Mike Tyson's career swept along like a slide show. Iron Mike walking a pet tiger in the grounds of his mansion. Tyson on his knees, gloves on the canvas, trying to gather both his senses and gum shield after being whacked by Jumbo Cummings. Evander Holyfield jumping like a petulant schoolboy after Tyson bit his ear and spat some of it out into the crowd. Does Tyson still keep pigeons? Tyson faded.

Saddam Hussein loomed. Mark recalled a news item that showed Saddam performing a light hearted jig in front of other leaders. Another showed him shooting his rifle into the air when his troops marched past with their heads turned to face him on parade. The bemused look on Saddam's face when George Galloway visited and described him as 'indefatigable'. Saddam, unshaven and unkempt, discovered living underground whilst on the run. Saddam being led to the gallows by angry men in balaclavas and filmed by phone as he swung. Mark had read somewhere that Saddam liked to feed birds in the prison yard. Where were those birds now? It occurred to Mark that his own interest in birds gave him something in common with Iron Mike and Saddam Hussein and this made him smile. The bus passed the train station and the next stop was Mark's. The shop opened at nine but Mark got there much earlier to start his jobs. He had a key and worked on his own until opening, when the owners, Mr and Mrs Grayson, came down from the flat to supervise.

Mark opened the front door, walked into the shop and locked up again from the inside. It smelt of animals, sawdust and faeces. Various creatures scratched in anticipation of food. Air bubbles in the fish tanks gurgled. Mark turned the lights on and went to the storeroom in the back. He had plenty to do so reluctantly hung his coat up and started straight away on the morning tasks, cleaning out cages, feeding, restocking shelves. He checked the rota, which kept him up to date about tasks that necessitated a strict schedule. Two guppy tanks to drain and the resident boa constrictor, Rosy, to feed.

Mark enjoyed feeding the snakes and liked to take his time and watch carefully. They were supposed to be fed defrosted dead rodents, but he didn't see the point. Nature is brutal, he reasoned, and if the snakes were wild they would eat live animals. He went to the fridge, took a defrosted mouse, wrapped it in newspaper and placed it in the bottom of a bin before peering into a large glass mouse cage. One of the mice arbitrarily caught his eye and, after stalking its movements, he lifted it by the tip of its tail. The mouse hung with its claws stretched, trying to turn its head, but unable to properly move. Mark studied it closely; the whiskers, the pinkness around the eyes, the soft fur, the squeaky panic.

He narrowly opened the top of the glass vivarium and Rosy looked up, curiously thrusting her forked tongue. Mark dropped the mouse and closed the top before swiftly kneeling on one knee so he could watch through the glass. The mouse sensed danger, scuttling to the opposite end from Rosy and anxiously twitching. Rosy unfurled her body and hovered towards her prey. She was so alert, so curious, and so hungry.

When Rosy's head was about three inches away the mouse rushed back to the other side of the vivarium and this time hid behind a water bowl. Rosy's movements were swifter and more vigorous now as she followed, peering in an elevated position. Having stalked she was ready to eat. Mark was careful not to blink. In one furious lunge Rosy caught the body of the mouse behind its head in her teeth, applying relentless pressure whilst coiling to constrict the final residue of life.

Mark watched carefully. The face of the mouse got larger, eyes imploring, teeth protruding, tail twitching. After a minute or so Rosy let go and moved herself into a position to feast. She lowered her bottom jaw and started to swallow the mouse whole. Its tail looked like it was swaying slightly as it entered head first before disappearing completely into Rosy.

Mark smiled and started to blink again. Standing up, he set about getting the shop ready for opening. He turned on the till, made sure it had receipt paper and filled up a few half full shelves with dog food, fish flakes, flea lotion, books about budgies, pottery treasure chests and shipwrecks. After starting to drain the guppy tanks he reversed the closed sign and opened. It was nine o'clock, and Mr and Mrs Grayson entered promptly, appearing through the doorway at the back of the counter.

'Have you fed Rosy and drained the guppies?' asked Mr Grayson.

Mr Grayson stood behind his wife with raised eyebrows while waiting for Mark's response. About a month ago Mark had forgotten some tasks off the rota and was reminded of his oversight every morning.

'Yes. I'm working on the guppies,' Mark wearily replied.

'Right. Carry on then,' demanded Mr Grayson sternly.

The Graysons had been best friends with Mark's late parents and had given him a job because they promised to. Therefore he should be eternally grateful. No one else would have him, hence the attitude. Mark didn't like them, had hated his parents and, besides birds and Rosy, didn't really like animals either. The Grayson's thought Mark was 'not a full shilling'. Mark knew because he heard them mutter it so often.

Mr Grayson kept a close eye on Mark that morning like every other, making a point of inspecting his watch. Occasionally he spoke: 'Do you have any gears other than first?', 'Have you finished draining those guppies yet?', 'Don't you have a decent pair of shoes lad?' Mrs Grayson heard the last comment and slowly shook her head. Customers popped in for supplies. Mark scooped three guppies and two bala sharks for a middle-aged lady, put them in separate clear plastic bags with tank water and took them to the counter. He cleaned out the gerbils, the budgies, the rabbits, the mice and the rats before taking all the rubbish out. Time crawled, but 12.30 came and Mark asked the Graysons if he could go for lunch. Mr Grayson ordered, 'Be back at 1.15 sharp.'

Mark eagerly fetched his coat, left the shop and meandered

around the corner to Jean's pantry for an all-day breakfast. As he walked in he had a good look at the other customers and was surprised not to recognise them. There was a table near the counter with two workmen in bright yellow jackets tucking into big plates of fried food, laughing raucously. Two other customers sat separately. One was an elderly man reading a tabloid whilst holding a hot drink, and the other a middle-aged woman with folded arms gazing out the window with her cup steaming on the table. Mark ordered, paid at the counter and took a vacant table near the door where he could appraise the customers clearly. With cautious ceremony he slipped off his coat and hung it over the back of a chair occupying the facing seat.

He studied the workmen's faces. One was about fifty, bald except for a few tufts on the sides. Mark considered him with thoughtful contempt. He probably had children, a son and daughter in their early twenties. A wife who works at Tesco. Holidays in Spain or Turkey. Sky TV. It's possible he likes fishing and the mortgage is nearly paid off. Things are getting easier. Loves his kids. Maybe the daughter went to university and got a 2.1 in Media Studies. Her graduation picture sits in the middle of the mantelpiece. The son could be in the army and stationed abroad. A picture of him in full uniform sits next to the one of his sister. Mum and dad are so proud.

The other workman was possibly in his late twenties. Mark gave him a life too. Soon to be married. Football at the weekends, Manchester City. Reads *Four Four Two* and the *Daily Mirror*. Fancies Jordan and Beyonce. Loves rock music. Recently mortgaged to the hilt. Fatherhood around the corner.

The elderly man. Born just after World War II. Wife died. Keeps mind and limbs active. Loves crosswords and cares for sick sister. Feels vulnerable. Struggles to pay council tax and hopes his property is not sold to cover his care. Would rather die. Two daughters need the cash.

The middle-aged woman. Married to childhood sweetheart since late teens, but bored. She's thinking about another affair. A younger man at work is willing. Sex still interests her, but her husband has become fat and dull. There is a huge gap between how she hoped her life would be and how it has become. Kids have just left home and she's frightened and excited by the change.

Mark's food and tea arrived, jolting him out of his reverie. He anxiously added two sugars before putting a thin layer of mustard over the sausages. How he wished he could get out of the habit of giving people backgrounds. It served no purpose other than to make his plans seem more necessary. And what useless lives they lived; no sense of destiny, churning out the dull years. Futile, all of it. Head down, he chewed slowly before placing his coat back on and returning to the shop.

He treated fish tanks, cleaned more cages, signed and checked a small delivery. The Graysons said nothing. Customers came and went. Mrs Grayson sold a budgie to a lady from church. Mark hoped it would be cared for. Mr Grayson stayed behind the counter taking the money, reading the paper, answering the phone. The shop stayed open until 5.30, but Mark always finished at four. When that time came Mr Grayson nodded gravely, stating, 'OK you can go. Make sure you're on time tomorrow. We've got an early delivery.'

Mark headed straight to the storeroom for his coat. The weather had cleared so he decided to wander to the park. A large weeping willow stood in one corner and scattered throughout were barren horse chestnut trees and sycamores. He headed for a bench in a shelter that stank of stale urine and informed him that *Julie loves Steve 4 ever* and *MUFC rule OK.* Sounds travelled. Traffic hummed and a horn beeped. Far away small children played on swings and he could hear laughter and shouting.

His thoughts turned to his life and what it had taught him. People want power. His own father had ruled the house with an iron fist. Mother had ruled Mark under the guise of love. Dictators rule countries and subjugate people forcefully if challenged. Liberal democracies do the same, but are usually more subtle and use the illusion of freedom to subvert resistance. Life is a battle for scarce resources and everyone wants more. More food, more money, more property, more credit, more froth on cappuccinos. Industries exist on the basis that people can be persuaded they need what they don't have. Belief systems grip and guide people who are frightened of floating alone in a void. People have minds that question life's meaning. Some think they have answers.

Lives follow similar patterns through generations: birth, school, romance, careers, children, houses, holidays, rows, divorce, grandchildren, retirement, ill health, death. On and on until an enormous comet shoots out of the sky and smashes into earth sending everything, frothy cappuccinos and magnificent cities, out into space as if nothing had ever happened. What is left will be fossilised for millions of years in another galaxy and discovered by an alien species looking for resources.

He'd read somewhere a description of infinity as being like a sparrow flying to the peak of a mountain every hundred years, scraping its beak on the top and doing so until the mountain is worn down and the bird can start on another. His own miniscule existence during forever encouraged a feeling that he must do something to overcome his insignificance. The Graysons were right. Maybe he wasn't a full shilling. He was glad. That thought kept him alive, along with the belief that only he understands how meaningless life is. It was this, he was convinced, that made him unique, superior and with a destiny to fulfil. He was both the chosen one and the chooser.

Mark left the park to catch the bus home. It started raining again. The forecast had been spot on. He got on the bus and sat behind two girls swearing about the state of their fake tans and 'dickhead fellas'. A teenage boy with headphones stared nonchalantly at the empty seat opposite. Every now and then he tapped his foot to the rhythm and this irritated Mark, but he was unsure why. He pulled his coat in close and his heart briefly accelerated. Someone had written 'Fuck you' in large letters through the condensation on the window. He scrubbed it away and watched his journey go past in the dying light. Here the railway station, there a football pitch, a school, a church, stretches of open road and home.

He walked the short distance to his front door, opened, went in and hung his coat carefully back on the stand. Adolf the mynah greeted him so he fed and watered the bird and told him he loved his pretty boy. He made beans on toast and ate to *The News at Six* before reading *A History of Public Executions* for a bit and settling in to watch *Coronation Street*. It was time for a bath before washing the dishes. The evening slipped by uneventfully and he watched *The News at Ten* in case some atrocity had occurred within the last few hours.

At 10.30 Mark went to the coat stand and gently reached into the inside pocket for his silver handgun, feeling its contours lovingly as he took it upstairs to his bedroom. He turned off all the lights, opened the shutter window slightly and knelt. People were coming in and out of the pub opposite. There's Mr Carter the old P.E teacher. No need to invent a story for him. He had a stroke last year and drinks heavily. Wife left him. Lives alone, but regularly sees his son, an engineer. Mark aimed the gun at Mr Carter's head and kept that target until Mr Carter was safely inside. Soon, out came two overweight giggling young women with white legs, short skirts and bleached blonde hair. A quick guess. A hairdresser and a trainee beautician. Hard core dance fans on the way to Pete's fish and chips. Mark aimed his gun in turns at them until they were out of sight. Sluts. Not a single woman had ever taken a romantic or sexual interest in him resulting in a build-up of ferocious, unanswered desire equalled only by resentment. He carried on for half an hour aiming at people, giving them lives with his angry finger on the trigger silent in the darkness. He had been doing this for two years and the temptation to pull was reaching breaking point.

At 11.05 Mark switched on the light. He nipped downstairs and said 'Goodnight sweet angel' to Adolf. Upstairs, he folded next day's clothes and put them on his chest of drawers, placing a pair of balled-up socks on top. All the clothes were new, bought especially. A nice new pair of shiny brown brogues waited in the wardrobe. He set the alarm and wondered about breakfast. Country crisp. Something special for Adolf.

Mark turned off the lamp, closed his eyes and smiled. The next day was going to be special. And the gun? A plastic toy from Poundstretcher.

A Visit Home

I hadn't seen my Uncle Bryn since leaving town shortly after leaving school and there he was standing at the bar in The Blue Bell making a couple of quarry men laugh with one of his stories. Seeing him like that awakened a few memories. When I was ten my Dad left and it was Uncle Bryn who kept an eye on Mam, me, and my younger sister Beth. Sometimes he took us to the pictures or a local match at weekends and we'd walk home along the riverbank eating chips and playing I spy.

Mam used to enjoy his visits. She'd beg him to do one of his impressions and laugh every single time. It was good to see her like that. As we got older he would talk to us whenever we had been in trouble with Mam or at school. Try to 'steer us in the right direction', as he put it. Everyone looked up to him. He helped run a local football team and had a good job with the Council. In our family he was a hero. His wife, my Aunty Dilys, had agoraphobia so we only saw her when we went to their house, which wasn't often. Mam said Aunty Dilys was funny about visitors and the house smelled something awful.

I went up behind Uncle Bryn, tapped on a shoulder and said 'Guess who?' He turned and looked at me intently.

'My God, Dylan,' he said, throwing his arms around me and shaking my hand, 'great to see you.'

'And you Uncle Bryn.'

'Forget the uncle. Just Bryn now you're older. Let's sit down and catch up,' he said warmly.

'Okay,' I replied.

We found an empty table and eyed each other. I'd grown a beard, my hair was long and I wore a gold earring in my left ear. I could sense disapproval but he didn't comment. He had more greys than I remembered, but otherwise it was the same old Uncle Bryn. Well dressed, flabby and affable.

'How long have you been home?' he asked.

'A few days.'

'I spoke to your mam on the phone the other night. She didn't mention you were coming home,' he said.

'I didn't tell her. I rang Beth to make sure it would be alright. Mam only came home last night. She was at Aunty Gwyneth's for a few days. I surprised her.'

'That's right, now you mention it she said she was at Gwyneth's. Ah, Beth. Doing well with her A-levels apparently. What are you up to? Your mam says your training to be a… what's it called?'

'Psychiatric nurse. One year left to qualify,' I said.

'Good on you. You'll never be short of work that's for sure. The world's full of nutters.'

I smiled faintly. 'You can say that again,' I said. Uncle Bryn seemed happy with the response. Boundaries were coming down.

'Still support Wrexham?' he asked.

'As always. Went to the cup match at the racecourse last week. We still lump the ball up the pitch and chase after it. Doing well though. Might make the playoffs this season,' I said.

'Maybe. We need a proper striker though. Someone with twenty goals a season in them.'

'True. How's your team coming along?' I asked.

'I don't coach anymore. Dilys needs a bit of looking after these days. Dicky heart. I do a bit of fund raising. Keep my hand in.'

'How's work?' I asked.

'I'll be glad to finish to be honest. It's a load of nonsense. Nothing but cut backs. I'm half hoping for redundancy or even early retirement,' he said.

He went on to ask what it was like to be back in town,

if it had changed. I told him things were mainly the same. The new extension on the old school building looked good, but I was sorry the red telephone box had been taken down near the old post office, which I hoped would stay open. He told me it would close over his dead body and that he was collecting signatures and a petition to that effect. Next came a rant about local goings on.

'Did you hear about the swans down at the reservoir?' he asked.

'No.'

'Some cruel swine has only gone and decapitated one of them for God's sake. John Saunders the sparky found it yesterday when taking his dog for a walk. A terrible mess. I've informed The Herald and it will be on the front page next week. Disgusting,' said Uncle Bryn.

I thought about the swans. When Dad was around we would sometimes take a walk along the reservoir when the nights were light after tea. Beth would come too, collecting small flowers in a jam jar for Mam on the way. One night Dad pointed at the newly arrived mute swans. 'I admire swans so much son. Shall I tell you why?' he asked.

'Go on. Why Dad?'

'They're monogamous,' he said.

'What's mimogamus Dad?'

He smiled. 'It means the mummy and daddy swans stay together forever. They don't run off with other swans.'

'They grow old together Dad?'

'That's right. Also, they both build the nest and take it in turns to protect their young too. Noble creatures, Dylan.' He taught me how to tell the difference between males and females that same night.

Dad left soon after. Beth and I didn't know where he'd gone. Mam cried for months and said all sorts about him. He'd run off with someone else, we should just forget about him, he's no good. She stopped laughing, became lonely and aged quickly. After a short while we weren't allowed to talk about him. I grew to hate the woman he ran off with whoever she was and I tried to hate my dad too but I missed him. I'd wander over to the reservoir sometimes to see the swans and think about him. A mute son who couldn't speak about or to his father. My dad couldn't be like a swan and I asked a teacher what 'noble' means.

Whilst I was thinking about all that, Uncle Bryn was talking about how the pair of swans had been together at the reservoir for years and that the one left behind would surely die of a broken heart. I half heard and registered disapproval, shaking my head.

'Has the sex of the swan been established? It's not easy to tell the difference between a cob and pen,' I said.

'It was the male. A chap from the R.S.P.B. came to take it away and identify it. Whoever did it should be strung up,' Uncle Bryn said, using a hand to demonstrate a noose around his neck.

I nodded again and went back to half listening. Uncle Bryn moved on to other examples of bad local behaviour in order, I sensed, to demonstrate his heightened indignation. I was thinking of the grieving swan left behind but Uncle Bryn was now outraged by a recent spate of tyre slashing. Apparently, youngsters had been targeting streets and slashing two tyres on each car parked on whichever road. Most people didn't have two spare tyres so the inconvenience and distress was considerable. The answer, Uncle Bryn insisted, was CCTV everywhere and national service.

Sensing I was preoccupied he progressed to other things.

'How do you find your mam?' he asked.

'Find her? What do you mean?'

'Well how does she seem? Is she alright?' he was watching me carefully.

'Seems fine to me. Same old Mam. Shopping, bingo, cigarettes and crosswords. A bit quiet,' I said.

Uncle Bryn paused and then we spent the next hour falling over ourselves to pass opinion on current affairs. Wars, celebrities, the economy, sport. Uncle Bryn knew a great deal and held firm views. We ended up talking about films.

'Have you seen *The Damned United* yet Bryn?' I asked.

That was the first time I had ever called him Bryn and it didn't feel right. It was too informal, but I needed to do it at least once.

'Yes I saw it. Bit harsh on Don Revie I thought,' he said.

'I know what you mean. Hell of a character Clough though. Mam used to love that impression you did of him,' I said.

'Now you listen to me young man!'

I laughed. Uncle Bryn had Clough's nasal twang just right. The subject of films always excites me.

'I went to one of the best films I've ever seen recently,' I told him.

'What was that?'

'*Slum Dog Millionaire*. Loved it. The story, the music, everything. Saw it twice. Have you seen it?' I asked.

'You must be joking. Why'd I watch a film full of Pakis? Not interested,' he said.

'Oh.'

I didn't know what to say. I had no idea Uncle Bryn was like that. I was getting tired and decided after a little more chat that it was time to leave.

'Well, good to see you Bryn. I'll tell Mam I saw you. Best to Aunty Dilys,' I said.

'Okay Dylan. Don't be a stranger. Pop by and see us. Love to your mam,' he said.

'Sure. Bye.'

We shook hands and I ambled home. On the way I felt a little disillusioned. Uncle Bryn was no longer a hero, just another flawed human being. My mam was still up when I got home and that surprised me. She's always been early to bed. She made us both a mug of hot chocolate and sat on the couch with me whilst I watched the News. A foreign correspondent was reporting riots in a far off land when she chirped in, casually, 'See anyone in The Blue bell?'

'Yeah. I saw Uncle Bryn. He sends his love.'

'Oh, did you speak to him?' asked Mam.

'Yes. We had a few drinks together. Caught up,' I said.

'Well, has he changed much?'

'Not really. Same old Bryn. He doesn't want to be called uncle anymore,' I said.

'Did you tell him about your girlfriend?' asked Mam.

I knew what Mam was getting at. She must have known his views on 'Pakis'.

'No. Maybe he could meet Hansika next time. I could bring her here.'

'Err, yeah why not?' Did he mention anything in particular?'

She was getting at something, but I just carried on. 'Oh, we talked about all sorts. Football, the swans at the reservoir, the tyre-slashing epidemic, current affairs, films. Lots. We sat and chatted for about an hour,' I told her.

'Did he mention anything about your dad?'

'No. What about him?'

'I'm sorry love. Your Aunty Gwyneth got in touch and that's why I went to stay. I've been waiting for the right moment. He's died. I told Uncle Bryn and Beth that I'd tell you.'

'When? What happened?' I asked.

'On Wednesday. A sudden heart attack, complete surprise,' said Mam.

'Where was he?'

'He was living in a flat with his partner in Birmingham,' said Mam, a hint of judgement to her tone.

I turned off the news, muttered about it being a shame and asked Mam how she felt. She burst into tears and said she had loved him and was so sorry he died despite everything. He was, after all, the father of her children. There was to be a funeral in a few days and I could go if I wanted. Beth had decided not to go. I gave Mam a hug and stayed with her for a short while. When she seemed better I went to bed. It was strange simply going to bed so soon after hearing news like that. Disrespectful somehow. I imagined a lone swan flying dream like in slow motion upwards in an open azure sky and then I fell headlong into a deep sleep.

When I woke I couldn't stop thinking about the swan left behind. It was very early so I placed my clothes on softly and crept downstairs, grabbing a slice of bread from the kitchen and putting it in my coat pocket. Outside in the back yard it was still quite dark and cool as I prised open the crumbling shed where Dad's old garden tools still hung on rusty nails. I took down the machete he used for cutting back undergrowth and placed it in an old green canvas back pack that hung from a vice handle before heading for the reservoir.

I returned home to find Mam smoking in the living room and doing a crossword. She asked me where I'd been so early. I told her I couldn't sleep so took a stroll down to the church yard to meditate. Mam thought I must be hungry by now and she asked if I fancied a round of toast. I said I did, but that I'd make it. Dad had died and here I was eating two rounds of white toast with ginger marmalade. His favourite breakfast. It was my idea of a send-off.

I Drink Therefore I Am

I'd had a simple Sunday. A roast beef dinner with Helen, my wife, and a walk with the dogs around the lake and through the park. Early in the evening I suggested a quiet drink at our local but Helen didn't fancy it so I took the newspaper for company.

The Hunter's Bugle stands near a stream that flows past our village. The sort of pub where the same people stand or sit in the same place and some keep their own pint glasses behind the bar. Strangers are clocked. Darts, pool, brass ornaments, open fire, wooden beams, real ale and regular bar staff. As I approached I noticed that the old sign of a traditional huntsman in faded red, blowing his bugle astride a galloping horse, had been replaced. The new sign was comical. The heavily moustachioed hunter was fantastically portly and both the horse and bugle tiny in comparison. Inside I spoke to a few regulars before ordering a pint of the latest guest ale, 'Olde Familiar,' from Lucy the barmaid. Then I headed for a favoured corner table to quietly read the headlines.

The Government was behind in the polls and the world was filled with trouble. Normality. The beer tasted sour and warm, but notably fortifying. As I was about to turn to the sports pages I sensed someone moving towards my table. I looked up and before me was an oddly familiar, rotund man. He held a glass of red wine and his deportment was a bit stiff and superior. Across his upper lip he wore long thick dark whiskers that gave him the humorous appearance of an ancient walrus. Tersely, he asked if he could join me. I hesitated. There were plenty of other places to sit and I didn't want to be disturbed.

'Well?' he demanded.

'Yes of course,' I replied, hiding my resignation.

I folded the newspaper and put it to one side, preparing myself for the kind of inconsequential chatter I'd hoped to avoid. He sat in the chair opposite, inched forward so that our heads were rather close and looked me straight in the eyes for a few seconds.

'Who are you?' he asked.

'My name is Richard. Friends call me Richie. You can call me Richie.' I offered my hand with a smile.

He studied my eyes without expression and ignored the hand. I turned away to look around. Everyone was just getting on with what they were doing. Fumbling with the edge of my paper I felt foreboding. I should have stayed at home with Helen. He kept his gaze.

'I didn't ask for your name. My question was who are you?' he said.

'Well, I live locally and I'm a plumber,' I told him.

He moved his head back a little and that was some relief. I wondered if I'd given him too much information. Would he be able to find out where I live? I took a sip of my pint to appear calm and returned his gaze. He looked as though he was studying the essence of who I am. A long minute passed. I backed down and looked around because I wondered if people would consider the two of us gaping at each other peculiar but again no one was taking notice. I also felt he could see something in me that was not solid, something insubstantial. I looked back and his eyes still pierced. He moved forward again.

'So, your name is Richard. You live locally and you're a plumber. Is that it? Is that *who* you are?' His tone was dismissive.

'Is this some kind of joke? Has someone put you up to this? I'm just trying to relax for God's sake,' I said with some force. He didn't flinch.

'Keep God out of it. Who are-?'

'The question, pal, is not who I am. The question is who are you? I don't know you, that's for sure and you sit here asking me stupid questions,' I said.

He stood up and looked me up and down with contempt. 'OK. I'll leave. You don't know who you are,' he concluded.

With that he turned and waddled slowly out of the pub without drawing so much as a glance from the normally curious locals. Shortly afterwards I could just about make out a distant bugle call. I sat thinking back on the encounter before ringing Helen.

'You'll never believe this. A complete stranger approached me tonight and kept asking who I was,' I said.

'Did you tell him?' asked Helen.

'Yes. Well kind of. I told him my name and that I live and work locally.'

'So what's the problem?'

'He still said I don't know who I am.'

'How odd. You do know who you are. He was probably some weirdo or drunk.'

'Maybe. Back in a few. Love you honey.'

'And you.'

I drank up, wandered home and watched a bit of television with Helen before bed. I couldn't sleep. I kept asking myself 'Who am I?' Just who is Richard Morgan? Who is anyone? What does it mean to define yourself as this or that person? Am I Richard Morgan? I could have been given a different name. Would that change me from being who I am if I lived exactly the same life? Hardly. Surely a name is just a handy identification. It just tells us what someone decided to call us. And what of all the other people called Richard Morgan? They are not me. This went on all week. A plumber? Could have been a carpenter. Lives locally? Could have lived in the next village. Who am I?

The following Sunday I went back to The Hunter's

115

Bugle at the same time, taking Helen along and hoping to see the man again. I wanted to question him, find out if he knew who I was, but he wasn't there. Neither was the new sign, the old one was back in place and Lucy looked very confused when I asked for a pint of 'Olde Familiar' and enquired if she'd seen a portly man that looks like a walrus. She knew nothing of either.

Thereafter, at odd times I'd think about his question. It could be half time at a football match, fixing a blocked pipe, eating dinner at home, lying in bed. Who am I? Sometimes I'd think I had found a breakthrough, but it wouldn't last. Suppose we are just physical. That's what we are. This body is who I am. But then I'd think a bit harder. This body is not the same as it was when I was a boy, as all the aches and pains make clear. We deteriorate. And it changes all the time. I read somewhere that every cell in the body dies and is replaced over and over in a lifetime. Am I this body now? The past body? The future body? Could part of my body, say my brain, be put into someone else's body one day? What then? Would I still be me, or just part of who I am? Is the brain who we are?

At other times I'd think about my mind. The opinions and principles I hold are what make me who I am. However, I realised my views often depend on the newspaper I read, the programmes I watch on television, the people I talk to. All things pull me this way or that to form views which change frequently, often beyond recognition. I've changed the way I vote down the years. My outlook on religion and the possibility of an afterlife changed as youth's certainties slipped away. And what of personality? I'm not even the same person with different people. I show my best side to customers and they get an ideal sense of who I am. As soon as I get home I'm someone else. 'Mr Grumpy' is Helen's favourite name for me. Everything fluctuates and changes.

Anyway, maybe the fleeting mind is just a brain function, but how could something invisible like a unique thought of mine come from that? What is the self? One day I really thought I'd cracked it. Who am I? I am the person who has uniquely experienced this life and holds these memories of it. This is who I am and it is what makes me unique. This kept me happy for a while. Then I remembered my Aunty Flo. Towards the end of her life she couldn't remember much, even who her close relatives were. If we forget what we once remembered, how does this make the idea of who we are stable? What of those forgotten experiences? When Aunty Flo was in her prime she sometimes picked me up from school and took me somewhere as a surprise. The Science of Industry Museum was our favourite. I would be mesmerised as Aunty Flo knew about the history of the industrial revolution, what was made, how it was made and where in Britain. She taught these things at a local college. My Aunty Flo was an amazing and zany woman, a fun aunty to have. Which person defined her? Aunty Flo in the past or the later version?

I started to read the great philosophers past and present but still couldn't find a convincing answer to the stranger's question. Some years later I was returning some books at the local library desk when I heard the call of a bugle. No one else heard it, but I felt compelled to turn around and look towards the entrance. A familiar portly man with a walrus moustache was staring at me, through me. It was my turn at the desk so I kept the encounter brief before heading straight to where he had been but there was no sign of him.

I ran outside and through the streets before spotting the walrus man as he was just about to board a bus. I shouted loudly, 'Excuse me. Do you remember me? We spoke once in The Hunter's Bugle about...'

He ignored me and boarded the bus. As it drew away he looked out of the back window, waving and smiling knowingly until out of view. Elusive, in transit, beyond reach. Just like me.

The Ghost Orchid

My Granddad was a steam train driver. The family albums are full of fading black and white pictures of him standing on the footplate, often with his fireman. He looks like a portlier version of when I knew him, with his tummy stretching the buttons of his mucky overalls, big black boots and grubby slanted cap. He drove on the Southern Railway until the mid-60's when steam was being phased out so he retrained to drive diesel and electric trains. These were cleaner and faster but Granddad loved steam with a passion.

When he retired, we often sat in his shed and talked about his career. He started off cleaning steam locomotives in gangs of six, eight hours for each engine, using oily paraffin cloths to get the wheels and pistons clean before raising the fire for the fireman. He was a fireman himself for a few years, shovelling coal into the fire box. Coal from Yorkshire was best, he'd always say. I've still got some of the diagrams he drew whilst explaining the workings of steam locomotives; intricate little pencil sketches of boilers, pistons and cylinders. When he started driving trains he worked a route that took him past his house and he would sound the whistle as he approached the crossing stile. Sometimes Gran would surprise him and turn up waving and he'd blow the whistle as he went past.

During the school holidays Granddad and I used to wander over to the old line, scaling that same stile with his grimy old work bag full of sandwiches and a flask of tea made by Gran. The track was mainly hidden by brambles and nettles by then but could easily be exposed. On our last visit he took me some way down the line and uncovered some track by removing the foliage.

'This is where I'd blow the whistle for your Gran,' he said.

'How would you know it was here, this exact spot?' I asked.

'There was a whistle board on the side of the track to tell us to warn the public of an oncoming train. It had the letters SW on it meaning sound whistle. It stood directly opposite the church steeple, so when I was going past it I'd blow,' said Granddad, pointing to the village church. 'We were only allowed to blow our whistles when it was necessary. Rules and Regulations were very strict.'

'When else could you blow it?'

'Mainly to warn railway workers that a train was coming or at stations to indicate that a train was about to move. That sort of thing. We used codes, long and short whistles for different situations.'

'Was it the same as the whistles referees use at football matches Granddad?'

Granddad chuckled, cuffing one of my ears playfully before explaining that a lever was pulled, opening a valve that allowed steam to escape which in turn created the sound. He promised a drawing or two back at the shed and stood there for a moment looking up and down the track with his hands on his waist. We then headed for the woods behind the track to look for birds. Treading carefully and moving slowly we listened out for woodpeckers, cuckoos and willow warblers and I spotted a tree creeper through my small binoculars.

We also liked to find wildflowers on our ramblings and over the seasons we'd sit and eat our sandwiches whenever we found favourites such as foxgloves, snowdrops, honeysuckle and old man's beard. I loved those names and on this day we sat on a tree stump surrounded by weird fungi and some nearby wild butterfly orchids. Granddad was particularly fond of orchids.

'Do you want me to tell you a secret?' he asked.

'Go on Granddad. I won't tell anyone.'

'About fifteen years ago I came up here, not far from this spot, and found a ghost orchid.'

'A ghost orchid? You mean it was a wildflower ghost?' I said, uneasily.

Granddad laughed heartily and then spluttered a bit on his spam sandwich, wiping his mouth with his oily cuff. 'Not exactly, but that's what they're called,' he said.

'If it's a flower and you found it, why is it a secret?' I asked.

'Ghost orchids are the rarest flowers in Britain. Decades can go by without them being seen. If too many people knew the location they would take them away. Best to tell people who are really interested in wildflowers and understand the need to keep quiet about it.'

'Did you tell anyone?'

'Well, first I made sure I knew exactly where I'd found it but I had to go to work that afternoon for the night shift. The next time I had a chance I came back and brought my camera with me. I wanted to see it on my own again. My heart was fair thumping I was so excited. It had gone though. I never saw it again. I told the local wildflower society and took the chairman to the exact spot and that was the last of it. Out of habit I still look out for it in the area around the sighting. Obviously, I told your Gran too.'

'What do you think happened to it? Surely it didn't disappear like a ghost,' I said.

'I've no idea what happened to it. The chairman said they flower rarely and then only for a few days. Conditions have to be just right. If I hadn't had to go to work that day I could have been a part of ghost orchid history. A young girl found one in the 1920's apparently and there have been a few other sightings but that's about it. It's almost impossible to spot. The one I found was tiny and it was

121

camouflaged amongst the beech leaves in a dark part of the woods at the end of summer.'

'What do they look like Granddad? I'd love to see one.'

'They look like something you'd find on another planet. No leaves, a pale stem and a white flower that looks like a spider. I've got some drawings of them in my wildflower book. We can take a look later.'

'Let's go to where you found it. You never know.'

'Well, we can go and have a quick look but don't get your hopes up. It's a bit early I think to find one but there's no harm in looking.'

With that we wandered off to the exact spot but had no luck despite going on our hands and knees to gently forage around the leaves. After half an hour we gave up and sat against a beech tree to drink tea.

'I want you to promise me that you'll pop here every now and then when you come to these woods through the years. Have a look around in this area, though I've no reason to believe they sprout up in the same place. Just a hunch I have,' said Granddad.

'I will. But what about you? You'll be with me,' I said.

Granddad looked thoughtful for a moment. 'I won't be here forever Danny and it's unlikely you'll find one but if you do I'll be smiling down on you wherever I am.'

'Alright Granddad I promise. Will you promise me you'll live a long time though? I can't imagine coming to the woods without you.'

He laughed and ruffled my hair. 'I'll do my best lad. I promise that.'

Late afternoon we left the woods, crossed the tracks and stile and headed home. Gran had made my favourite, cowboy dinner, a stew made with beans, meat and lots of potatoes.

'I thought you two had gone to Timbuktu,' she said when we walked in.

'We've been looking for a ghost orchid Gran,' I said.

'Your Granddad told you about that did he? I'm still waiting for the evidence,' Gran said, winking at me.

'I tell you it was there clear as day,' protested Granddad.

'Well, if you go upstairs you'll find a clean shirt on the bed. Prove it exists by wearing it for tea,' said Gran.

Granddad slumped upstairs to get changed and that cowboy dinner tasted even better with home-made bread, butter from the larder and a side plate of pickled red cabbage from the allotment. After tea, Granddad and I went to the shed and he drew some diagrams to illustrate how a steam train whistle works and showed me a drawing of a ghost orchid from his oily and battered copy of 'Wildflowers of Britain'.

That was the last time I saw Granddad. Shortly after that visit he became really poorly and died a few months later. He had been unwell for some time apparently. My parents said it would be too upsetting for me to see him deteriorate or go to his funeral as I was only ten years of age. I was still able to stay with Gran during the holidays and did so as soon as the term ended.

'Why are you ironing Granddad's old shirts Gran?'

'I miss him love. It makes me feel close to him. I still wash and iron his clothes and put them back in the wardrobe. Habit I suppose. Mind you, it's impossible to get all the muck off his collars and cuffs.'

'Can we take a walk tomorrow to the stile where you used to wave at him when he drove past?'

'That's a good idea love. I'll make up a flask and some sandwiches. What would you like on them?'

'Spam please Gran.'

We sat on the stile the next day and Gran waved as if Granddad was driving past. I took her to the place where

Granddad had seen the ghost orchid too. Over the years we took the same walk at least once during the holidays but we never did find the flower.

When I was much older I continued staying with Gran whenever I was working in the area and kept my promise by visiting the woods. She gradually lost the ability to walk unaided and was often in and out of hospital with various ailments. My mum stayed regularly and a home care team made frequent daily visits. There was talk of a nursing home but Gran wanted to hang on as long as she could in the house she'd shared with Granddad.

'I'll be pushing daisies soon that's for sure. When your Granddad was ill he said he'd blow his train whistle twice when it's my turn. That's why I'm hanging on. When I hear that I'll know he's come for me and my time's up.'

The situation reached crisis point. Mum was talking about quitting her job to look after Gran, who was by now in her nineties. Hospitals stays increased and for longer periods. Even Gran was coming round to the idea that a nursing home might be considered.

'I suppose I'll go when I have to but they'll sell this place to pay the fees,' she said.

All of this was churning through my mind on a visit to a heritage railway with my wife Maria and our children Sophie and Oliver. It was a late summer afternoon, perfect for hurtling through the countryside on a steam train. We bundled off the train at its destination and straight into the railway shop. I liked a steam train poster which Maria said she would frame and put in the living room and the kids chose some colouring books and a Thomas the tank engine DVD. I was having a good browse whilst Maria and the kids queued up to pay. I was still in there when the family went out to the platform to see the latest train arriving so I bought a toy and hid it in my jacket thinking I'd surprise everyone with it later. It was only when I was driving home that I devised a plan.

Two days later I drove down to Gran's house, arriving quite late. I parked up the road and watched the last carer of the day leave. I knew that Gran would have just gone to bed with help from the carer and that she would still be awake, possibly reading. Gran wore reading glasses but her sight and hearing were relatively good for her age. I used my key very quietly, entering with stealth, leaving the door on the latch. Gran was in her bedroom with her door slightly ajar and a book in front of her on a moveable table. I retreated back a few steps and took the toy from the railway shop out from my jacket pocket. I blew hard into it twice, each a full breath, so that a loud imitation steam train whistle pierced the stillness. After the second whistle I retreated promptly to the front door. 'Is that you Alf?' Gran softly asked as I took the door off the latch and left furtively.

The next day I got a call from my mother. Gran had been taken into hospital that morning and it was touch and go. The morning carer had found her drifting in and out of consciousness, whispering something about a train whistle. The hospital staff felt that Gran may not leave as indications suggested she may not pull through. I took the day off work and dashed down the motorway but Gran had died by the time I arrived. Mother said she had seemed almost happy when she'd been awake, holding and squeezing mum's hand with a radiant smile. The train whistle was mentioned a few times and Gran said over and over that her time had come. There was a message for me, one of the last things Gran said. She wanted me to look for the orchid. She was buried next to Granddad in the church that he had used as a sign to blow his whistle for Gran in the days of steam.

I struggled for some time after Gran died. I was coping

125

with bereavement of course, but also a terrible guilt that I had brought about Gran's death prematurely. Had I committed a soft murder? I didn't talk to Maria about it and I took the train whistle to a charity shop with a bag of clothes. Most of Gran's estate had been passed down to my mother but our family had also inherited a useful sum of money. Years went by, the kids grew up and went to university and I kept the secret of the whistle within my heart. I put it to the back of my mind mostly, but every year I'd feel contrite whenever I visited my Grandparent's graves to place some butterfly orchids on the anniversaries of their deaths. After each visit I felt compelled to go to the woods and look for the ghost orchid just in case. One year, Maria joined me. The old stile was still there and we clambered over it. I showed her the old railway line and the place where Granddad blew his whistle.

'Amazing to think she heard it again just before she died,' said Maria.

We walked into the woods and spotted some birds before arriving at the place where Granddad had found the ghost orchid. I'd shown Maria pictures of ghost orchids over the years, these being more common now with the internet. We set about searching on our hands and knees. We were just about to give up when I spotted a petite, leafless plant about six inches tall, almost transparent amongst the camouflage of beech leaves but there in front of my eyes with a single white flower on top. I stared at it for a moment of wonder before looking upwards through the trees and whispered, 'Granddad I hope you're smiling up there.'

I caught Maria's eye and beckoned her over and we sat in a kneeling position like prayers at church. We found ourselves whispering, keeping obsessively still and distant enough not to breathe on the flower, barely breathing in the musty aroma of the earth and leaves. Carefully, I took out my phone, put it in camera mode and took half a dozen pictures zoomed in from different angles. Getting up we took it in turns to move our knees quietly backwards before standing. We headed back through the woods, over the stile and back to the car, agreeing not to tell anyone at this stage. That night after tea I thought about nothing other than the ghost orchid. It was a sign from my grandparents that I had done the right thing and the guilt dropped from my shoulders. I sat in my study for hours just looking at the pictures on my phone. Maria thought they were really good, though I noticed we both lowered our voices again whilst viewing.

A couple of days later I went back to the woods. The ghost orchid was gone and a part of me was pleased. It was as if my grandparents had sent a message on that day only. On the way home I popped into the local camera shop to get the pictures developed. The ghost orchid pictures came up on the screen quite clearly, so I ordered them in normal size and enlarged because I wanted to choose the best for framing and putting in my study. I arranged to pick them up in a week as I was out of town on business in the meantime and Maria had a hefty schedule herself.

Upon collection I resisted the longing to look at them straight away and, once home, put them on my study desk in their envelopes ready for Maria to join me when she came home. She was as excited as me after tea when I told her where they were. We rushed upstairs like children, sat together and opened the normal size envelope first.

With sacred care I placed each picture on the desk and we sat hunched over in anticipation. The pictures had come out in fine detail, decaying beech leaves in crisp glorious colour but no ghost orchid in any of them. We did the same with the enlarged pictures but still no ghost orchid. Maria suggested I look at the pictures on my phone as we had that same night after they were taken. I zoomed in on each one but there were no ghost orchids to be seen. We sat there in silence unable to account for it. Maria eventually said that maybe we were so excited on the day that we'd imagined it. 'Both of us?' I countered. A few days later I went back to the developers and they still had the pictures on file. No flowers. Maria and I recounted the story to numerous friends when out to dinner on occasion but stopped when we realised people thought we'd simply made a mistake, that we'd thought we'd seen something but hadn't, there was no mystery. We even started to believe it ourselves as time passed.

Some years later I decided to put all my photographs in new albums as the binding had gone on the old ones. I enjoyed looking at all the old pictures and put them back in loose order depending on theme; holidays, birthdays, Sophie and Oliver's graduations and so forth. One collection was for steam trains and in these I put the old photographs of Granddad in his mucky overalls on the footplate of his train alongside pictures of the kids on the day we went to the heritage railway.

Looking at those old pictures stirred within me a faint sense of recognition that I couldn't immediately put my finger on. There was a picture of the kids and Maria standing near the engine of the train that took us that day to the shop where I'd bought the toy whistle. The brass nameplate identified the train as The Snow Goose. On two of the pictures of Granddad the name of his train could be identified. The Snow Goose. I contacted the heritage railway with some enquiries and was told the engine had been restored and originally worked various lines including the one that went past the woods.

It was Granddad's old train.

Acknowledgements

First of all I would like to thank Gill James at Bridge House publishing for her kind and helpful editorial suggestions. I would also like to express gratitude with regards my late friend Mr Max Makin of Llandudno Writers who encouraged me when I started writing and proof read many of my stories. His friendly demeanour and open heartedness, along with his love for jazz and jokes leave me with happy memories.

Finally, I would like to thank my son, Oliver. I dragged him around many book shops when he was growing up and one day he said that it would be nice to see a book by his dad on the shelves. Here it is. I dedicate this book absolutely to him.

Other Publications by Bridge House

Other Ways of Being

by Gill James

Other Ways of Being is a an anthology of stories that point us to other times, other histories, other worlds including those of our near futures, other sexualities and other genders.

Order from Amazon:

Paperback: ISBN 978-1-907335-67-9
eBook: ISBN 978-1-907335-68-6

Because Sometimes Something Extraordinary Happens

by Debz Hobbs-Wyatt

Seventeen short stories by Debz Hobbs-Wyatt from over a decade of competition wins and shortlistings. Featuring *Learning to Fly*, winner of the inaugural Bath Short Story Award; *Chutney*, shortlisted in the Commonwealth Short Story Prize, and *Pushcart* nominated, The Theory of Circles.

Meet a mixture of beguiling narrators, from seven-year-old Leonardo Renoir Hope trying to change the past so his dad doesn't die, and George and his carrot-growing friends on an east London allotment waiting for the world to end, to Amy Fisher who realises that her husband, after his sudden death, is not who she thinks he is… but who is the other Mrs Fisher? This one adds a touch of medical horror to the mix.

All of the stories are about ordinary people when extraordinary things happen to them.

Order from Amazon:

Paperback: ISBN 978-1-907335-69-3
eBook: ISBN 978-1-907335-70-9

Links

by Dianne Stadhams

LINKS – sometimes random, many times unplanned, often with far reaching consequences, always shaping our journey from cradle to grave – the stuff of life.

Just how do Atta Gatta the child-eating crocodile, Scheherazade the pantomime star and Judy the stammering Goth strategically connect characters across the globe?

Enjoy this trilogy of inter-linked short stories that will make you smile and squirm as they raise questions about the needs and challenges of our contemporary world.

Order from Amazon:

Paperback: ISBN 978-1-907335-63-1
eBook: ISBN 978-1-907335-64-8

www.ingramcontent.com/pod-product-compliance
Lightning Source LLC
Chambersburg PA
CBHW071316130626
46556CB00004B/1630